TRANSFORMING ROSE

CATHERINE BANKS

TURBO KITTEN

Transforming Rose By Catherine Banks

This is a work of fiction. Names, characters, places and incidents either are the product of the author's imagination or are used fictitiously. Any resemblance to actual persons, living or dead, events, or locales is entirely coincidental.

Cover design by Covers by Combs.

Turbo Kitten Industries™, P.O. Box 5012, Galt, CA 95632

 Created with Vellum

Thank you to:
Jackie, for being a great fan and respectfully bugging me for more.
Professor Weinshilboum, for fostering my creativity in fiction writing class.
Avery, for being the Moon of my Life and providing me light in my darkest times.
RJ, for mentoring me and being an amazing friend. Your friendship means the world to me. Thank you for being you.

Prologue

Some acts scar us more than others. Some cruelties can never be forgotten. Some men should not be allowed to live.

And yet...

And yet there are those that torture, abuse, and neglect others, and nothing happens to them. The victims are forced to go on and attempt to repair themselves. I've learned that repair is not always possible. Sometimes you need another to help repair your broken mind and body. Unfortunately for me, those that could possibly repair me are also those that would hurt me more. Life was a cruel bitch.

Chapter 1

I stared at the obese Caucasian woman wearing a lime green dress, standing across the counter from me, and wished she would explode.

She was angry and wanted to speak to her lawyer *now*. I smiled at her as sweetly as I could manage.

"I'm sorry, ma'am, but Mr. Smith is in a meeting right now. I can take your name and number and let him know that you wish to speak with him, but he's busy at the moment. If you would like I could schedule an appointment for you to speak with him." I glanced down at the calendar in front of me for a moment. "He has Tuesday at three thirty available."

The woman glared at me, knowing I was irritated and dismissing her, but she also knew that she couldn't prove that Mr. Smith was really sitting in his office watching television and not in a meeting.

"I'll take the appointment," she said in a shrill voice.

I nodded. "Mr. Smith will see you on Tuesday, ma'am. Have a *nice* day."

She stormed out of the office, and I fought the urge to chase after her.

Stupid human.

I waited until she had waddled away from the building before I walked into the large office behind me. A fireplace that was never used occupied half of the left wall, while a large conference table occupied the right wall. The cabinet on the front wall could be opened to reveal a television and bar, which was used more frequently than anything else in the office. The office was decorated in warm red tones to try to soothe the clients' minds, but it only made me think of blood.

Richard Smith was a late-thirties, athletic, and somewhat attractive man. He knew the law better than he knew his own hands and he was the best lawyer in town. He turned away from the television and smiled at me as I came in. "Who was it this time?" he asked, guessing about my irritation, which was written plainly across my face.

"Ms. Lucille Shamus has scheduled an appointment with you for Tuesday to discuss her case," I said through gritted teeth.

Richard pointed to the seat across his desk, and I sat down in it. "You're always on edge this time of month. You need to lighten up, Rose."

I mumbled, "If your clients weren't such idiots I wouldn't get so upset."

Richard stood up and poured scotch into a glass with ice. He looked at me and I nodded. He pulled out a bottle of water and tossed it to me. I'm not a drinker because alcohol smells too horrendous for me to be able to drink. Richard smiled. "You always bring a smile to my face, Rose. Take the rest of the day off. I'll fend off the leeches today."

I smiled back at him and stood. "Paid day off?"

He laughed. "You've definitely been around me too long. Yes, paid day off. Now go on."

I left quickly, before a problem could come up or before he came to his senses. I started walking down the street and smiled as the irritation from the rude woman disappeared. It was a warm day for Northern California, but not hot, at least not yet. April proved to have fewer showers then it should, and now May brought a warm streak that didn't look like it was going to end anytime soon. Warm in California was better than cold or hot though. I inhaled the air and smelled exhaust, sewage, and blooming flowers. Sometimes having a good nose took away from the pleasantries of life in the city. I walked down the concrete sidewalk, ignoring the other people around me. Mondays were busy days for the downtown area and I reveled in the energy of those around me.

The crosswalk sign changed to the little white man and I walked quickly across, fighting the urge to skip in my giddiness. A man in his twenties started to walk by me and I caught myself checking him out. As he passed me, I caught his scent and all of my cheerfulness died. I kept facing forward, hoping he hadn't smelled me. I turned to look back once I'd reached the other side of the street and saw him standing in the center of the crosswalk sniffing the air, searching for my scent.

I turned back around and hurried to my house. My heart beat as fast as a hummingbird's wings as I fought the fear trying to overtake me. I slammed the door behind me and bolted it closed.

"Too close," I whispered.

It was the closest to another of my kind that I had come in over a month. I locked the three chains on my front door and smiled. It may not keep another of my kind out, but it would slow them down and alert me to their presence. I could be out the back door and hopping over the fence before they had finished getting into my living room.

I walked to the fridge and stared at the void where food should have been. My stomach growled loudly, reminding me that lunch had been missed and if I did not buy some groceries, dinner would be as well.

"Shit."

I needed food or I wouldn't be able to control myself. My control was already wavering since I could only afford a human's amount of food a month. I walked to my bedroom and turned my coin jar over, dumping the change on to my bedspread. I separated the coins and counted them quickly.

"Twenty-five dollars. It's enough to buy a few groceries."

I found an old purse and scooped the change into it, cringing at the loudness of the coins clanging together. I changed quickly out of my slacks and blouse and into hip hugger jeans and a *System of A Down* t-shirt. I checked my hair, and then walked out of the house carrying my change-filled, noisy purse.

I tested the air for any scent of the man I had seen, even though I doubted that he would have been able to track me in the city, but found none. Our noses may be good, but not that good. I waited at the crosswalk with two other women and felt their glares like a hand pressing against my side. Even underfed as I was, I still had a much better body than any of the average human women could attain. Fast metabolism and higher body temperature helped to keep my body at fifteen percent body fat constantly. I also ran every night to keep the jitters away.

The light changed and I walked past them, sashaying just a little more than normal to show off my curves. I knew I was attractive, with caramel brown hair, green eyes, and a swimsuit model type curvy body, but I usually didn't try to flaunt it.

That's what had gotten me into trouble before.

I walked five more blocks past old houses until finally coming to the grocery store. The grocery store was cool, and I released a sigh of contentment. I couldn't run the air conditioner as cold as I liked because I couldn't afford the bills. If I could have, the house would be closer to the arctic than the desert.

I poured my change into the coin machine and waited as it

counted it all. People milled about the grocery store and though I faced the coin machine, I kept them all in my peripheral. I could not afford to let anyone sneak up on me.

The receipt printed, I grabbed a shopping cart, and rolled it towards the first aisle.

Everything looked so good that I had to force myself to only grab the basics; meat, bread, milk and chocolate dipped ice cream pieces. The ice cream was my only vice and I didn't indulge often, but I was in need of ice cream after the close encounter with the male in the crosswalk. It was irritating how attractive the males were. If only they weren't such misogynistic, abusive jerks, I might be able to deal with them.

I walked to the cashier and put my items on the conveyer belt. The cashier was an average looking human, fit due to hours in a gym and strict dieting. He smiled at me and I smiled politely back. "Twenty-four dollars, please." His voice held a hint of a British accent and I reprimanded myself before I asked him to speak again. I was a sucker for men with accents.

"Here you go." I handed him the receipt from the coin machine and he handed me my change. I winked at him as I pushed my cart away. "Have a nice day."

I didn't usually flirt, but he was human, and I would never date one, so I figured, what the hell. Not like he could overpower me even if he wanted to. I grabbed my four bags and walked out of the grocery store, groaning when the heat slammed into me outside. My phone started vibrating, so I set the bags down and answered it quickly. "Hey, Richard."

"I have an urgent meeting tomorrow morning at eight o'clock. I need you here at seven o'clock to set up. There will be four of us and they'll be drinking water."

It was very unusual for him to set up a meeting this last minute, but I knew better than to question the boss. "It'll all be ready when you come in," I assured him.

He sighed and I could hear his nervousness. "These are *very* important clients, Rose. They are the ones that allowed me to buy my jet last year. I want everything to go perfect."

"I understand completely. I'll dress up and even put some makeup on," I said as seriously as I could.

He laughed softly. "Thank you, Rose. I needed that. I'll see you tomorrow."

He hung up the phone without saying goodbye or allowing me to.

"I hate waking up early," I muttered, put my phone away, and then picked my bags back up.

The walk back seemed to take twice as long, but that was just because of how hungry I was. I set my bags down at my doorstep and fumbled with my keys for a moment. The stench of foul body odor filled my nose and when I turned around, there were two bums eyeing my bags of food from the sidewalk in front of my porch.

I growled loudly and watched as their eyes widened in shock at my animal-like growl.

"Mine," I said.

They backed away slowly, before running down the road. I gripped the porch beam to keep myself from running after them. Never run from a predator. The humans never learned that lesson though. I felt my wolf settle down inside of me again and sighed. The moon was close to full and I would need to find someplace to change. I had found a few promising state parks, but everything was far away. I knew I would have to talk to Richard about taking some time off, but I didn't want to bring it up yet. I really hoped his meeting went well tomorrow so he would be in a good mood when I asked him. He had let me off every other time I asked, but then felt the need to remind me every day the rest of the month about having let me go. I'd learned to deal with it because I had to do it every month, but I still dreaded it.

After getting the groceries put away I made a human's

portion dinner and sat in front of the television to eat it. The crappy survival challenges were dominating prime time and I soon lost my desire to watch anything. I rinsed my plate off and changed into sweatpants and a sports bra. My tennis shoes were getting worn, but I couldn't afford new ones yet, so I slipped them on and prayed they'd last another week. The sun had set an hour ago and I knew it was my best chance to go for a run. I locked up the house and started jogging down the sidewalk towards the park.

Dogs barked from their pens nearby and I felt pity for their confined state. Living in the city was a sort of confinement for me, but nothing as awful as what domesticated dogs had to deal with. I needed the forest, the open land only confined by trees. That was heaven to me. I could have lived in the forest forever, but I hated hunters and decided to return to human cities. I had restrained myself for the past four years since becoming a wolf and not killed anything other than rabbits, squirrels, and the occasional cat. Man, did I hate cats. They were nothing more than stupid fluff balls of evil.

I inhaled and smelled trees only a half mile away. I increased my speed to a moderate run for a human and kept that pace as I ran through the park and underneath the trees. It wasn't the forest, but if I closed my eyes and focused really hard, I could pretend for a few moments. I made three circuits before a light sweat started to bead on my forehead. I could run longer, but I didn't want to be out too late and risk fighting a bum. I walked back towards my apartment basking in the moonlight. If only every night were as peaceful as this.

Chapter 2

The alarm buzzed next to me and interrupted my dreams of chasing cats in the forest. I growled and smacked it just a little too hard, smashing the snooze button.

"Dammit," I groaned, sitting up in my bed. I rubbed my eyes and stretched, feeling my bones cracking and my muscles stretching. After showering, I got dressed in the nicest outfit I had for work, a form revealing black and hot pink dress with a bow that tied on the side. It was sexy and yet still work acceptable. I grabbed the makeup bag from under the bathroom sink and started applying a thin layer to my eyes and lips. Once I was satisfied with my appearance, I slipped on my tennis shoes and grabbed my high heels. Although I could walk the ten blocks in high heels, I didn't want to risk breaking one of the shoes since I couldn't afford new ones. I walked quickly down the sidewalk and pressed my identification card to the pad, opening the front doors of the office.

The office was wonderfully quiet in the mornings and completely void of human life. I turned all of the lights on and set my bag down before walking to the conference room and starting to set up. A pile of packets sat on one end of the table so I moved the chairs around evenly and set one packet in front of each chair. I grabbed three bottles of water and set them down in front of three seats before starting the pot of coffee for Richard. He wasn't fully functional until he had a cup of coffee in the morning. The room smelled stale and even though a human wouldn't be able to tell, Richard said he wanted everything perfect. I grabbed the can of peppermint spray we kept under the kitchen sink and sprayed it around the room, just enough to be present, but not overpowering. Once I was satisfied that the room was set up perfectly, I rushed around the front office tidying everything up and spraying a little peppermint in the front as well. Richard walked in just as I was adding water to one of the flower vases.

He looked around the office then walked into the conference room and nodded his head. "Perfect. The peppermint is a nice touch."

I bowed my head at the neck. "Thank you."

He walked into his office and I made his cup of coffee, two sugars and one cream, and hurried in to give it to him. He sipped the coffee and sighed happily. "Delicious." He looked my outfit over and then at my tennis shoes. "Rose…"

I held up my hand and ran to my desk quickly changing shoes and hiding the tennis shoes in one of my drawers. I adjusted my dress and walked back into his office. "Better?"

He looked my outfit over again, smiled and nodded. "Great. You look very nice."

I blushed a little before I turned away and said, "Thank you." I shut his door so he could prepare for the meeting and sat down at my desk to wait for his clients.

I was staring longingly at the forest picture on my calendar beside my desk when a male voice asked, "You go to the forest often?"

I jumped a little and looked up at the handsome man standing in front of my desk. He wore a suit that hugged his shoulders, and a green tie that brought out the green in his hazel eyes. I hadn't even heard the door open or close. I inhaled and my throat instantly closed up at his smell. Shit. He was the guy from the crosswalk.

I shook my head. "Only been a few times," I whispered.

He smiled, showing perfectly straight, even, white teeth and I flinched. His smile wavered as he sat down in the chair across the desk from me. "I'm Mr. Wright, here to see Mr. Smith, but I'm a little early."

His hair was spiked, but somehow still looked professional. His eyes were mesmerizing and I wondered if his lips were as soft as they looked. Then I wondered how often he beat his mate for simply existing.

I recomposed myself and smiled politely at him, trying to keep from baring my teeth. "That's no problem. Let me go see if he's ready. Are you waiting for your other partners?"

He shook his head. "It is just me today."

I stood up slowly, and walked to Richard's office, shutting the door behind me and trying not to freak out. "There's a were…there's a man for your appointment here, but it's only one person. He said his name was Mr. Wright, I think."

Richard sighed. "I thought they might do that. Alright take him to the conference room and I'll meet him in there."

I swallowed my fear down and walked out of Richard's office. The man was staring at me with a genuine curiosity that frightened me.

"If you'll follow me, I'll take you to the conference room," I managed to say in a normal tone despite my nervousness.

He stood, and walked gracefully towards me. He was definitely a werewolf and he was *very* handsome. He looked close to my age, but it's always hard to tell someone's true age when they weren't human. As he came closer, I felt the pressure of his aura, like a hand against my back. He was a dominant, possibly an alpha. I dipped my head a little in a sign of submission and then led the way to the conference room. He followed five feet behind me and stayed quiet. My shoulder blades were itching fiercely by the time we made it to the conference room. He inhaled as we entered and I tensed to run.

He sighed happily. "I've always loved peppermint." He sat down in one of the chairs and I moved around him to grab the other three waters and packets. As I started to walk by him again, he laid a hand on my arm and I jumped sideways dropping the waters and packets. He frowned. "I'm sorry I didn't mean to startle you."

I squatted down, picking up the dropped items, and he squatted down beside me to help. He opened his mouth to say something when he inhaled and drew in my scent. His eyes widened and he looked up into my eyes. "You're a—"

I finished grabbing the waters and packets, and ran from the conference room. I knew it wasn't smart to run, but I had to get away from him.

Richard walked into the conference room, stopping Mr. Wright from following me. "Hello, Mr. Wright. It's a pleasure to see you again. Why don't we take a seat and discuss the contract?"

I put the waters away, put the packets on Richard's desk, and then grabbed my purse and ran out of the office as fast as I could.

Richard would have to find a new secretary, and I would have to move. I hated moving.

I made it two more blocks before I sat down and cried. I was so tired of running, and I didn't even have enough money to be able to move again. I couldn't let them catch me, but three years of running had exhausted me.

Someone grabbed at my purse, and I looked up into a filthy old man's gaze.

He only had three teeth and was snarling at me. "Hand it over and I won't hurt you," he said in a raspy voice.

I stood, and glared at the old man. "Back off. I am not in the mood."

He pulled out a pocket knife and flipped it open. "I was trying to be nice, but you had to push me."

I pulled my purse out of his hand and shoved him in the center of the chest, making him stumble backwards. People started slowing down to see what was happening.

I growled at the old man. "Leave before I lose my patience."

He screamed in rage and charged at me.

I stepped to the side to dodge his attack when a pair of hands grabbed the man by the throat and shoved him up against the wall.

The old man dropped his knife and held up his hands. "Sorry. Sorry," he gasped.

"Attacking a woman is hardly appropriate." The person holding the man up by his throat turned around, and I gasped at the golden wolf eyes staring at me from Mr. Wright's face.

I stepped back from him, dropped my purse, and ran away as fast as I could.

"Wait," he called after me.

I ignored him, thankful that I could disobey him even though he was a dominant. Fear and adrenaline aided my escape, and I made it home quicker than I ever had before. I looked around, and tested the air to see if he had followed, but I couldn't sense him. I pulled my keys out of my pocket, and groaned when I realized that I had dropped my purse back there. Hopefully, he would give it back to Richard, not that there was any money in there anyway.

I opened the door, and pulled off my heels before curling up on my bed, and pulling my blankets up over my head.

What did I do now? I needed to get away from him, but it was too difficult to relocate. Plus, Richard wouldn't give me a good reference if I just bailed on him.

I lay in bed for a few more minutes as I debated what my next move would be, when my stomach grumbled.

"Now I eat," I whispered angrily. I made a sandwich and sat in the middle of my bed eating it. The adrenaline finally dissipated and I felt a little shaky from the experience. I set the plate on the bedside table, and then lay down on my side again closing my eyes. I just needed to rest a minute, and then I would decide my next course of action.

The knocking on my door woke me from a dream, which had been peaceful, but now that I was awake, I couldn't remember what had happened. I groaned and sat up, wiping the sleep from my eyes. The person knocked twice again, and I stumbled out of my room. I checked my reflection in the mirror and frowned at the smeared mascara, which made me look awful. I wiped under my eyes, so I at least looked presentable, and opened the front door.

Mr. Wright held out my purse and smiled with his head bowed, trying to look submissive. "You dropped this earlier."

I jumped back from him.

He waved his hands. "Don't be scared. I'm not going to—"

I ran away from him, and towards the back door.

He was faster though, and appeared in front of the door frowning. "Just wait a second—"

I ran towards the front door, and he slammed it shut just before I got there.

I crouched down and snarled. "What do you want?"

He started to snarl back at me and then shook his head. "I just want to talk," he said in an almost whisper.

I growled again. "Who sent you? How did you find me?"

He scowled. "What are you talking about? No one sent me. You ran off before I could even talk to you. Now just *calm down.*"

I felt the pressure of a strange magic, like an arm reaching out to hug me, and gave in. I let the magic envelope me in a warm hug and gasped in surprise when the magic calmed me down. I had never felt a dominant use magic to calm before. It was surprisingly nice, but it didn't make me trust him any.

I backed away from him until I stood against the back door, still cautious. It was obvious that I couldn't run away from him, so I might as well calm down and think while he talked.

"What do you want?" I asked softly.

He sat down cross-legged in the middle of my living room floor and said, "I just want to talk."

It felt odd to be standing when a dominant was sitting, but I wanted to be able to run if I needed to. "Then talk."

He smiled. "What pack are you from?"

I shook my head. "I don't belong to a pack."

The smile changed into a frown. "You're solo? That's not allowed."

I felt my lip twitch and shrugged. "My ties were broken with my last pack."

He stared at me, silent, with wide eyes. "You broke your ties? Why?"

He seemed so sincere, so genuinely concerned that I almost told him.

I bit my lip nervously and said, "It's a long story, but basically my pack didn't treat me well. So, I left and broke my ties."

He frowned harder, and then I felt his anger like a warm wind ruffling my fur. He definitely had the potential to be an alpha if he wasn't one already.

"Is that where you got the scar from?" he asked with anger in his voice.

My right hand instantly went to my left wrist and traced the scar. I shook my head, speaking quietly, "No. This isn't from them. I did this."

He stared at me, eyes wide again for a moment before talking again. "Why don't you come with me to speak to my alpha—"

I growled and grabbed the door handle. "I'm not going back! I won't go back to them!"

He held his hands up in a sign of surrender. "Alright. Alright. Calm down. You shouldn't get so worked up this close to the full moon."

I released the handle and stared at him in complete and utter shock. "You're not going to take me back?"

He shook his head. "If you don't want to go, I'm not going to force you."

I sat down on the arm of the couch by the door. I didn't really believe him, but acting like a lunatic wouldn't help the situation. "So, why are you here then?"

He smiled. "To give you back your purse and talk to you. It's been a long time since I've met another werewolf outside of the pack meetings."

"Since we're not allowed to go solo, you mean? You're a born wolf aren't you?" I asked tilting my head to the side as I looked at him.

He frowned. "How'd you know that?"

I blushed and looked down. "The born wolves are always more handsome than the bitten ones. Plus, you're not attacking me and a bitten wolf as dominant as you would have already attacked me."

He shook his head. "That's not true. I know a lot of bitten wolves that are completely in control of their wolves."

I stared at him with narrowed eyes. "Really?"

He frowned. "Of course. Those that aren't in control aren't allowed out."

I shifted my butt and asked, "What do you want? I don't mean to be rude, but if you aren't taking me to my old pack or to your pack, then why are you here?"

He smiled and his cheeks turned pink. "I was actually hoping you would go out with me."

I tested the air for any hint of him lying, but he seemed to be telling the truth. I shook my head. "I can't. I'm sorry."

He stood up slowly and set a business card on top of my purse on the coffee table. "I don't know what happened with your last pack, but I would never hurt you. Please think about going out with me."

I watched as he walked out of the house and exhaled in relief. After staring at the business card for an hour I got up the nerve to call Richard.

He answered on the first ring, "Rose."

"I'm sorry Richard."

He laughed. "Don't be sorry. Whatever you said to that boy, he signed the contract and fronted half of the costs. You're getting a very nice bonus, my dear. Good job."

I stared at the phone for a moment. He'd signed because of me? No. "Well that's good. I need to ask you for a favor though."

Richard hesitated a moment. "Okay?"

"I need to take the rest of the week off."

"Right. I forgot that it was about that time of the month for you to take time off. Why don't you swing by the office in a few minutes and pick up your bonus before you go? Just in case you need it."

I hung up and pulled on my heels. I picked up the business card on top of my purse and read the name. "Sean Wright, specializing in all your personal travel needs." I slid the card into my purse and walked quickly to work. Maybe I would call him when I got back to at least apologize for being so rude to him. Maybe he really wasn't like the males from my last pack. I shook my head. No, male werewolves couldn't be trusted.

When I walked into the office, Richard handed me an envelope bulging with cash. "Don't comment or open it. Just be thankful," he said.

I smiled at him as I put the envelope in my purse. "Thank

you." I grabbed my tennis shoes and shut down my computer before walking back home. I looked around nervously, worried Sean would jump out and drag me kicking and screaming to his pack, but nothing happened. I packed what few things I needed and climbed into the car. As I drove out of the city and towards the mountains I began to feel calmer. It took three hours to drive to the specific part of the forest I wanted to run in, but I knew it would be worth it. I parked my car and stripped quickly out of my clothes before running into the forest. Being a werewolf had forced me to learn not to be modest.

The change was painful, but at the end it felt like a really good back adjustment. I stretched my four legs and wagged my tail. My wolf loved being free and I let her take over as we ran through the forest. Your wolf and you weren't two different beings, but more like you without human thoughts or inhibitions. She just wanted to run and hunt, whereas my human mind wanted to think about the problems we had encountered. To keep from letting her take over, you have to keep a harmonious balance between wolf and woman. If the wolf took over, she would go rogue, and hunting humans sounded like a fun dessert to rogues.

After tiring myself out running, I lay down in the leaves and sighed in contentment. I would spend the next four days in wolf form, only changing if absolutely necessary. A rabbit darted across the path in front of me and I jumped up, racing after it. After successfully catching and eating the rabbit, I found a patch of sun and lay down to relax. These were the best times of my life. No work. No werewolves. Just me enjoying my wolf form.

It would have been better if Sean was here, running with me, though.

I snarled and shook my head. No, I wouldn't think about him. This weekend was Sean free. Just me and the tasty small animals. I enjoyed this time alone. I was my own wolf. I was free.

Two days passed by quickly, but it was glorious to be able to run and hunt in wolf form. I crouched down as I spotted a herd of deer fifty feet in front of me. I didn't usually hunt deer, but I was in an adventurous mood. The deer hadn't seen me, and an older deer with a slight limp was closest to me, perfect to take down. A normal wolf wouldn't have been able to manage it, but as a werewolf I had more power than even a dire wolf and a bit more weight as well. I jumped from my spot and ran forward just as four other wolves ran at the herd.

No not wolves, werewolves. I turned away from the herd running to the right and hoping they hadn't seen me. I dodged around a tree and chanced a look back to see them chasing me now instead of the deer.

Shit.

I ran faster, weaving in and out of the trees and tucked my tail down as I heard them yip and bark to others of their pack. I heard responding barks in front of me and tried to alter my course, but a particularly large male jumped into the side of me, sending me head over tail. I landed on my stomach and hopped up with my teeth bared and my legs flexed, ready to run. The wolves encircled me, snarling and keeping me completely trapped. I cowered between them and tried to find an escape route. The wolf who had tackled me moved forward, growling angrily when a gray and black wolf jumped over the top of the others to stand between me and the large wolf.

I inhaled and stared at the wolf in disbelief.

Sean?

The gray and black wolf growled at the others and they all backed up. Another wolf walked forward and I felt his presence like being crushed by a car. Alpha. Sean bowed his head, but stayed standing in front of me. Bones popped and snapped and then a five-foot-six tall man stood in front of Sean. He looked around Sean at me and frowned. "What is this, Sean?"

Sean whined, yipped, and barked to the alpha, but I couldn't understand what he was saying. Unless you were in the pack with another werewolf, you couldn't communicate while in wolf form, even by barking to each other.

The alpha stepped around Sean to look at me. "What pack are you from, girl?"

I shook my head and pawed an "x" into the dirt.

The alpha frowned harder. "Change, so I can talk to you."

I looked around at all of the wolves glaring at me and whined. I didn't want to be in human form if they tried to attack me. Sean backed up three steps so that he was standing beside me and snorted. He nudged my shoulder and I shook my head. He was trying to show that he would protect me, but he couldn't protect me if the alpha ordered them to attack. There was an opening now that Sean had moved. If I took it, I could probably make it to the car before they caught up to me.

I shifted my feet nervously and the alpha sighed. "We aren't going to hurt you."

I'd heard that line before.

I bolted through the opening and past the alpha. I ran as fast as I could towards the car and heard only one wolf following me. I hoped it wasn't the brute who had tackled me earlier. I made it to the car and changed forms as fast as I could. Luckily changing was one of my talents and I finished in under a minute. I threw on a pair of sweat pants and a t-shirt just as Sean came in to view. He yipped at me and I climbed into the car, started the engine, and backed down the road as fast as I could. Sean stared at me from the road as I ran away with a look of confusion and sadness on his drooped head.

Chapter 3

I stayed in the house in my wolf form the rest of the weekend, but no one came. I decided it was probably safe and went to work on Monday morning. Richard left a pile of letters on my desk and I started photocopying them. Hours passed as I worked on photocopying the attachments to the letters, when someone came in the front door.

"I'll be with you in a minute," I called to them. No one responded, but some of his clients were rude like that. I finished copying everything and carried the stack back towards my desk. I stopped in the middle of the lobby and stared at Sean who was standing by my desk.

He smiled at me and sat down in the chair in front of my desk. "Hey, Rose."

I swallowed the fear down and walked to my desk, setting the papers down. "Mr. Wright. How can I help you today?"

He frowned at the use of his last name, but managed to regain his smile. "I've come to take you out to lunch."

I stared at him in shock. "What?"

"You didn't call me, but I assume that was because you were in wolf form most of the weekend. So, I decided that since I saved you in the forest, you would want to go out to lunch with me."

Blackmail, wonderful.

"I'm sorry, but—"

Richard walked into the office and his eyes widened. "Mr. Wright, I didn't know I had an appointment with you today." Richard glared at me accusingly and I fought the urge to flip him off.

Sean stood and shook his head. "No, actually, I'm here to take Rose out to lunch. We ran into each other this weekend and she agreed to go out to lunch with me."

I cleared my throat. "But as I was telling Mr. Wright, I know we have an *important* matter to deal with today—"

Richard waved his hand. "I can handle it."

That bastard knew what I was trying to do.

"You two go on. Take as long as you need," Richard insisted.

Sean was smiling smugly and I wanted to smack the smugness right off of his face. Sneaky bugger.

"Fine. One meal," I said softly.

Sean nodded to Richard. "Mr. Smith." Then, he walked to the front door and held it open.

I grabbed my purse and glared at Richard, who responded by smiling wider as I walked by. Sean led me down the sidewalk, which was filling up with people for the lunch hour. He stopped in front of a Mexican restaurant and held open the door for me. I stopped and looked at him, keeping my head down in submission and said, "One meal."

He nodded. "One meal."

We walked to an empty table and sat down. The waitress brought out chips, salsa, and cups of water. I ate the chips in silence while hoping that my fear wasn't right, that he wouldn't make me trust him just to send me back to my former pack. Sean watched me with curiosity in his eyes. I supposed that I should at least be polite since he was one of Richard's clients. "Thank you for helping me with the bum and your pack."

He smiled warmly. "You're welcome."

I looked at the small bruise on his chin. "You got in trouble because of me, didn't you?"

He touched the bruise on his chin. "I overstepped my place when I stepped between you and Ralph. He's beta in our pack and I shouldn't have done something so dominant towards him."

I realized I was reaching out towards his chin and pulled my hand back into my lap. "I'm sorry."

He shrugged. "They know better than to startle an unknown wolf like that. They shouldn't have ganged up on you like they did. Ralph got in trouble, too."

The waitress came over smiling at Sean. "How can I help you?" I don't think she meant with the food.

Sean nodded at me. "Beautiful ladies first."

I smiled sweetly at the waitress who was annoyed at the obvious sign from Sean. "I'll have two tacos and a side of rice and beans."

Sean frowned at me. "That's it?"

I frowned back at him.

He sighed. "No wonder you're so thin. I'll have six tacos and beans and rice. Oh, and add another three tacos to her order. Thank you."

I wanted to argue, but I really could use the extra food.

He looked me in the eyes. "I'm sorry, but you're too thin. Even in wolf form your ribs are showing. It's not safe or healthy for you to be so thin."

I glared at him. "It's not like I starve myself on purpose."

He smiled. "If you would talk to my alpha he could help you. The pack helps each other out." I started to stand and he put his hand on top of mine. "Don't go. I was just giving you a suggestion. Please. Stay."

I wanted to leave, but the pleading look in his eyes made me sit back down. Plus, it felt good to be near another wolf, even if I wouldn't admit that out loud. "I can't be in a pack. It doesn't work."

He shook his head. "We have females in our pack and they're perfectly happy."

I rolled my eyes. "Are you sure they are? Or is that what their mates tell you?"

He frowned. "Of course, they are. They have voices of their own. This isn't the *fifties*." He was so serious that it caught me by surprise. No wolf I had ever dealt with before spoke of women in a high regard. Women were just there for amusement, whether it be sex or torture, but not for friends or as *real* lovers. He rubbed his thumb across my hand and I realized he was still holding it. I jerked it back and ate a chip to hide my face. He asked, "What pack were you from?"

I swallowed the chip and asked, "Why does it matter? I broke the ties and I don't want to go back. I'll die before I go back to them."

He exhaled and the soothing magic spread over me, like pulling up a warm blanket in a cold room. "Let's talk about something else. Why did you pick this city?"

I shrugged. "Our kind don't usually like the cities so I figured I wouldn't run into many here." Sean was very attractive even for our kind, his thick black hair was spiked again and his hazel eyes shone in the lights. Why was he talking to me? "Isn't your mate going to be mad that you're talking with me?" I asked.

He shook his head. "I don't have a mate."

I stared at him, wide-eyed. "So, are you one of the ones that date human girls?"

He looked disgusted, as though he vomited in his mouth at my question. "No." He seemed to understand my questions and smiled. "There aren't many free females around—"

The waitress brought us our food, which interrupted him.

He waited until she left and smiled wider at me. "I'd really like to get to know you better."

I stared at him for a full minute before my brain finally began to function. "I don't know if I can give you what you want." Dammit, that's not what I meant to say. I meant to say no.

He shook his head. "All I want is for you to give me a chance." He pointed at my plate of food. "Eat."

I shook my head. "You're more dominant and…" He raised an eyebrow and the look was so sexy and breathtaking that I found I couldn't argue. I started eating my tacos and he started eating with me. We ate in pleasant silence and I felt safe for the first time in years. Dominants can make a submissive feel completely safe just by their presence. Whether the dominant could really protect you or whether they wanted to was another matter altogether though. I chastised myself mentally for letting my guard drop with him and allowing myself to be so attracted to him. It didn't matter how much I craved a mate, I knew it didn't work. I knew what pain they could inflict.

We finished our food and started walking back to my office. He didn't talk until we were standing outside the door. "Come out with me tonight."

I shook my head and backed away from him, preparing for his anger when I refused. "I'm sorry, I can't."

"I don't know what happened with your last pack, or how they treated you, but not all of us are bad," he whispered softly as he looked down at me. "Lumping all males into the mean jerk category is like lumping all human males into the psychotic, serial killer category. A few does not represent the many."

I knew he had to be right, but I couldn't chance it. I couldn't go back to the way it was. "I'm sorry."

He exhaled softly and looked sad. "You have my number,

so when you decide that you're tired of playing the lone wolf, call me. If you want, we could go running together. No strings attached. Just a nice evening run."

That sounded like the greatest thing ever, but I couldn't be alone with him. I wasn't sure how he had controlled himself this long as it was. I couldn't risk him losing control and beating me or worse.

"I'll consider it," I whispered.

He knew I was lying, he could smell it. He stepped towards me and my body shook with fear. He inhaled my scent and whispered, "Have a good day, Rose."

I watched him leave and then walked on wobbly legs into the office.

"What happened?" Richard asked.

I shook my head. "Nothing. We ate lunch and he asked me out, but I declined."

"You declined! Why would you do that?" Richard asked, his mouth agape.

I glared at him. "It's none of your business. I just don't like guys like him." Only that wasn't true. I craved the companionship of another wolf, especially a male, alpha wolf. It was hard being a lone wolf.

Richard threw his hands up in exasperation and walked to his office.

Humans. They were all just focused on two things, money and reproduction. They didn't understand what it meant to survive; to endure pain and torture at the hands of the ones you couldn't help loving. Every day was torture for me.

Except today. Today with Sean near me had been pain free and nice. Of course, that would all stop once he gave up the charade and started beating me.

He *had* saved me from his beta, though. That could just be part of his ploy. I groaned angrily and focused on the work at my desk, trying to forget about him.

As the clock ticked over to five I hurried out of the office and home. I continually checked the air, but never found his scent or any other of our kind around. I made a small meal and finished the evening by watching television and eating ice cream.

Why was he being so nice? He had seemed angry when I made a comment about their females. Was his pack different? Did his pack actually treat women with kindness? There was only one way to find out, but I couldn't go to his alpha without risking being sent back to my old pack. *That* would not happen. I would sooner die than go back to them.

I felt twitchy, so I changed into sweats and tennis shoes, and jogged down the street. People milled around on the streets, some already intoxicated as I jogged by. The blare of music spewed from the open bar doors. I watched as scantily clad women paraded in front of the human men and felt jealous. I'd been just like one of them, until Jeff had found me and bitten me. I shouldn't have ever caught his attention. I should have trusted my instincts and stayed away from him, but he was a tough guy and that had excited my stupid human brain. Plus, he'd been great to me while I was human.

Now I wished that I could take it all back. Never met him. Never became a werewolf. Never have fallen in love with that psychotic jerk. Even now part of me missed him. I firmly believed it was just my wolf side missing a pack, but if I really analyzed my feelings, I knew it was because of the mating bond. I still hadn't quite figured out how to break that. There had to be a way, though.

My nose picked up a scent, and I slowed as I came to the corner. I saw Sean with two other men, both obviously werewolves, too. Sean laughed at something his friend said, and then turned and met my eyes. He was handsome, and I desperately wanted to be near him again. He smiled at me and started to move towards me, but I turned around and ran. I couldn't let myself fall for another man. I couldn't let him take control of my life like I had let Jeff.

I made it home and locked my doors as quickly as I could. The locks wouldn't stop them, but it made me feel better.

I showered and climbed into bed. There had to be a solution. There had to be a way to test him. Surely, I could think of some way to make him show his true intentions. I had spent a lot of time in therapy to become able to even exist in the human world. My therapist told me that the last step was accepting exactly what Sean had said, not every man was bad. Could I do it? Could I let myself fall for another male? Could I make myself vulnerable? I had escaped my last pack, so it was possible I could escape Sean if he captured me and hurt me. I wasn't as weak as I had been when first turned.

A run with him was the perfect idea to test him. I was faster than most males, so if he became threatening, I could just run into the forest and make a trail no one would be able to follow. Yes, that's what I would do.

I fell asleep dreaming of running through delicious bunny-filled fields with Sean by my side.

Richard was unusually grumpy the next morning and no joke I made helped his mood. I finally broke down and walked into his office. "Okay, what's wrong?"

"You. I just can't believe you turned down a rich, hand-some guy like Sean Wright. Do you know that women are always vying for his attention, but none ever gets it? You, however, caught his attention and you turned him away. I just don't understand."

I knew why the women never caught his attention. Humans were not ideal mates for werewolves. They either freaked out when they saw you change, or did stupid human things that irked the wolf within. Plus, our wolf could never be happy with a human.

"Well for your information, I'm calling him tonight to go out. So, you can stop being so damn crabby and cheer up."

Richard sat back in his chair and steepled his fingers. "Why the change of heart?"

"Not that it's any of your business, but I've had a bad track record with guys like him turning out to be psychopaths. So, I'm going to give him a chance to show his true intentions."

"Sounds smart to me."

I rolled my eyes. "Glad my plan meets your approval."

He smiled and waved me out. "Go call him."

I shut his office door and walked to my desk. I'd planned on waiting until later to call, but now was as good a time as any other. I pulled the card from my purse and dialed the phone number.

"Sean Wright, travel agent."

"Hi, Sean. It's Rose."

A chair creaked on his end and he said, "I wasn't expecting you to call after last night."

I felt embarrassed and was glad that he wasn't here in person to see my face. "Yeah, I'm sorry about that. I was just scared your friends might make me go to your alpha and I will *not* go to him."

"So, why are you calling?" he asked suspiciously.

"I wanted to take you up on your offer for a run. There's a park about thirty miles away that's big, full of small animals, and is unused by humans. We could change and run in it. That is, if you still want to." My stomach felt like it was tied in knots.

"Of course, I want to. What time? And do you want me to pick you up?" he asked excitedly.

He seemed genuinely happy. Or he was acting again?

"Seven o'clock, and you can meet me at my house, but I prefer to drive myself."

"Still don't trust me?" he asked sadly.

"I don't trust any wolves."

"Alright, I'll see you tonight."

"Okay."

"Rose, I'm really looking forward to tonight. I'm glad that you called."

I smiled at the affection in his voice and said, "Me too."

I hung up the phone and groaned loudly, thumping my head down against the desk. What the hell was I doing? If he ended up being like Jeff, I was going to have to run away all over again. I hated running away. I was tired of running away.

"Didn't go as you'd planned?" Richard asked from behind me.

I sat up and sighed. "It went exactly as planned."

"And that's a problem?" he asked quizzically.

I put my head back on my desk and whispered, "I don't know."

Richard patted my back reassuringly and said, "Just give him a chance. He could end up being the sweetest, most perfect guy you've ever met."

"Or a psychotic rapist who gets his kicks by torturing me."

Richard laughed. "You've definitely had some bad relationships. Rose, I've worked with Mr. Wright for three years and he's always seemed like a good guy. Sure, he's a little different than most people, always commenting on smells and weird things like that, but overall, he seems like a good guy. Remember, this is coming from a lawyer."

I laughed and sat up. "Thanks, Richard."

He nodded and handed me a large file. "Now, make two copies of this and hole punch them for me. Thanks."

I took the file and smiled at him as we returned to our normal work relationship.

I finished work, changed clothes, and stood on my porch, anxiously waiting for Sean. Part of me hoped he wouldn't show, while a larger part of me couldn't wait to run with another wolf, especially one who wasn't *hunting me*.

Sean stopped in front of my house in an older truck and smiled at me as he climbed out. "Ready?"

I nodded as my fingers dug into my arms. "I'd like to set some ground rules first."

Sean nodded. "Okay."

"Play is okay, but if I yip, you back off. I only hunt small animals like rabbits, so no taking down any deer or anything large like that. And absolutely no mating."

Sean smiled. "Sounds good to me."

I nodded and climbed into my car. Sean followed behind me as we made our way out of town and towards the large park. It took half an hour, but we finally made it and my nerves were completely frayed. I climbed out of my car and walked deep into the trees. Sean followed me silently, not even making noise with his shoes. I wished I was as stealthy as him.

I stopped at my favorite place to change and turned to face him. The moonlight highlighted his hair and face, making him look like an angel. A very sexy, muscular angel. "Okay. I'm going to go behind this bush to change. I don't like people being near me while I change. I'll yip when I'm done."

He nodded and walked to another bush across the way.

The change was painless and I took a moment to stretch in my preferred form before yipping and stepping around the bush. Sean walked towards me and I admired his wolf form. He dropped the front half of his body down and wagged his tail in an invitation to play. I snorted and spun around, running into the trees. He yipped in excitement and caught up to me quickly, running next to me.

I spotted a rabbit and was preparing to pounce on it when Sean snapped it up in his jaws and shook it. He dropped the rabbit in front of me, but I snorted and shook my head. I would not accept food from him. Not this early on.

Sean whined and nudged the rabbit towards me. I pushed it with my foot back towards him and took off after a squirrel that had tried to dart past me.

I trotted back to Sean who was eating his rabbit and ate my squirrel. Sean wiped his muzzle with his paw as he waited for me to finish and studied me. His eyes roamed all over me as I ate and even though I knew it was dumb, I felt naked. I finished eating and sat down on my rump, meeting his eyes. Sean suddenly leapt at me and knocked me over. I yipped in fear and he jumped away, tilting his head sideways in question. My heart was racing as fast as a cornered rabbit's and my body shook in fear.

He dipped his head down and crawled to me on his belly in submission and apology. He lifted his head and licked the bottom of my jaw.

Never before had a male werewolf apologized to me. I stood and faced him, my head now tilted in question as I tried to understand him. Was it a ploy or was he just sorry for frightening me?

Sean whined and licked my jaw again before backing away and standing up. I didn't know what to do. How do you acknowledge an apology? I bobbed my head up and down in a yes and then stood on my back legs before pushing on his back and knocking him to the ground.

He huffed and bit my front leg, but kept his teeth away from my skin. I pulled my leg out of his mouth and ran away, pausing when I was a reasonable distance away and wagged my tail happily.

Sean's tongue lolled out the side of his mouth and he sprang after me in excitement. He tackled me and then ran away. I tackled him and then ran away. We played until we were too tired to move and then lay down on the ground side by side. It was the most fun I'd had since becoming a werewolf. I wished time would freeze so I could enjoy this moment forever, but I knew real life would come back and bite me in the rump.

Sean stood and stretched, flicking his tongue over my muzzle. I stood as well, and we walked back to our clothes and got dressed.

Sean waited by our cars, looking nervous. "I'm sorry I scared you at first."

I shook my head. "Don't apologize. It wasn't your fault."

"Will you go out with me tomorrow night?" he asked as he met my eyes.

I opened my mouth to give him the automatic rejection I was so used to giving, but I *did* want to go out with him again. It felt right to be with another wolf. Plus, he'd held up to his end of the bargain and we'd had a great time together. "Where?" I asked.

He smiled. "Dinner and dancing."

I nodded. "Alright, but you have to promise me that you won't take me to your alpha."

He nodded, smiling wide. "I'll pick you up at six." He bent down quickly and kissed my cheek before climbing into his truck and driving away. I watched him leave and put a hand up to touch the place he had kissed.

Maybe things could work with him. He didn't seem like the others. Of course, they'd changed after I did, but I was already a wolf and Sean still liked me. Was that the key?

Chapter 4

I walked into the office and found Richard sitting at my desk, twirling one of my pencils. "So?" he asked.

He had never come into the office this early ever in his life. "My life outside of the office is not your concern, but if you have to pry I'm going out with him again tonight."

Richard smiled wide. "That a girl. You need some money to buy some clothes to wear? My treat."

I stared at him with wide eyes. He had always been nice to me and understanding of my monthly trips, but this was abnormal. "No thanks. I have clothes to wear and besides I just got to work."

He shook his head. "Never look a gift horse in the mouth." He pulled out his wallet and handed me two, one hundred dollar bills. "Go buy something nice to wear. In fact, go over to Perfectly Proper. I have an account there and I'll get the girls to help you find something." I opened my mouth to argue and he pushed me towards the door, tossing my purse at me. "Go on. Consider this work related since his happiness could help my bank account."

I walked out of the office and towards the mall grumbling

about overbearing, nosey bosses the entire way. The mall was packed, even though it was a work day and I dodged and moved my way through the crowd. I finally made it to the uppity clothing store Richard had suggested, and a woman stood smiling at the entrance. "Rose?"

I nodded.

She waved me in. "Let's find you something to wear."

To my surprise, they actually had some cute trendy clothes, not just snobby clothes. After arguing about three different outfits for thirty minutes, we both agreed on a figure-hugging black dress which was short enough to draw attention to my legs, but long enough that I wouldn't be giving everyone a show while dancing. Another thirty minutes of arguing over shoes, and then we moved on to jewelry, easily coming to an agreement on the dangling black earrings I found on the shelf. I grabbed the bags and window shopped throughout the rest of the store before going back to my house. It was five o'clock by the time I got home, giving me one hour to get ready. I quickly showered, changed, and applied the appropriate amount of makeup to bring out my eyes without smelling like chemicals.

I still didn't fully trust Sean, so I used a piece of tape to secure a knife to my upper thigh where it would be hidden even while I danced, but still there if I needed it.

I felt Sean's presence moments before he rang the doorbell. I double checked my appearance, my knife, and grabbed my ID before walking to the door. I took a cleansing, steadying breath and opened it.

Sean was wearing a pair of designer blue jeans that hugged his muscular legs and a blue collared shirt that clung to his upper chest and biceps, highlighting his muscles nicely. He wore some type of cologne that was noticeable, but not over-bearing. His hazel eyes appeared mostly blue, with the shirt bringing out that color. He was handsome and I found myself instantly enthralled by his smile. He held up a bouquet of red roses and spoke softly like you would to a scared animal, "You look stunning."

I took the roses from him and inhaled. "These smell great. Let me put them in water."

He shook his head. "Our dinner reservations don't give us much time. They'll last until we get back."

I wanted to argue, but I'd learned never to argue with a dominant. I set the flowers down on the table by the front door and smiled at him. "Alright."

He extended his bent elbow to me, and I slid my hand into the crease of his elbow. The presence of such a dominant male touching me woke my wolf up and put her on edge. Sean kissed my cheek softly and whispered, "Shh...I won't harm either of you."

His magic calmed my wolf and she settled down into a peaceful sleep. I sighed happily and whispered, "I've never met a dominant who soothes like you do. It's nice."

He frowned at me. "You've never had a dominant that soothes?"

I shook my head. "Nope."

We walked in silence for a few minutes as I enjoyed the scent of wolf, forest and his cologne that had a hint of peppermint in it.

Sean asked quietly, "Will you tell me about your former pack?"

I stopped walking and looked at him. "Why?"

"I want to know everything about you and knowing about your former pack will help me get to know you. Plus, if I know what happened, I can avoid frightening you like I did last night."

"I prefer not to talk about it." Or think about it.

"How about we make a deal?" he asked with a glint of mischief in his eyes.

I pushed the mental images of men beating me bloody out

of my head and folded my arms across my chest. "Like what?"

He tapped his chin in thought for a moment then smiled. "If you truly have a good night and I don't make any advances towards you, you'll tell me about your pack."

A nice night and no sexual advances? He was good at bargaining. "Alright, it's a deal."

He smiled that dazzling smile of his, and put my hand back in the crook of his elbow. We walked ten more blocks before stopping at an expensive Italian restaurant. He spoke to the hostess and then we were led to a small booth in the back corner of the restaurant, away from the humans.

The waiter took our orders as soon as we sat down and Sean asked, "So, how do you like working for Mr. Smith?"

I shrugged and tore off a piece of bread. "He's a great attorney and the pay is okay. Downtown is just expensive for rent so my food allowance is smaller than I need. The work is easy enough, but dealing with the humans is hard sometimes."

He nodded as he listened and then asked, "What do you do for fun?"

I shook my head. "I don't do anything. I just work, go home and go for a jog at night. I find it's easier to stay away from the humans as much as possible now that I'm solo."

He looked into my eyes and I saw worry. "Have you had any incidents?"

I shook my head. "No, but I want to keep it that way."

Our food came out and I frowned at him. "This came here really fast."

He smiled. "I gave the chef and his wife a really good deal on their travel last year." I waited for him to start eating, but he raised that sexy eyebrow again. "We're equals here. You eat at the same time as I eat."

I stared at him in complete disbelief and shook my head. "We are not equals. I'm female and you're male. I'm submissive and you're dominant."

He laughed loudly, shaking his head. "You are *not* a submissive." He stopped laughing and whispered, "Besides males and females *are* equals." I opened my mouth then closed it. He pointed his fork at my pasta and chicken and whispered, "Please eat."

I took a bite of my pasta and moaned. "This is delicious." I managed to stay silent the rest of the meal, finishing the pasta, chicken and even the bread on the table. Sean asked if I wanted seconds and I shook my head. "No. No, I'm fine."

He wanted to argue, I could see it by the frown that formed, but he just agreed, "Alright."

Point for him.

He paid the bill and led me from the restaurant to the dance club. The bouncer checked our IDs over three times before finally letting us in. As a werewolf, the aging process slows in your twenties and stops at the humans' fifty-five. Sean led me on to the dance floor and the music pulsed through me, drowning out my senses so that only the beat of the bass through my feet kept me on beat. Sean danced next to me allowing distance between us and I smiled. Another point for him.

Graceful and talented were natural to werewolves and we soon found a rhythm to dance together. I moved closer to him and he smiled wide. He kept his hands to himself, which earned him yet another point.

The humans watched us with growing envy and it made me smile wider. My throat was dry and I pointed to the bar. Sean nodded and held my hand loosely as we walked through the crowded dance floor to the bar. He ordered two waters and handed me one. He opened his bottle and began guzzling the contents down. A few drops slipped out of his mouth and slid down his throat. The desire to lick the trail up was so intense that I had to turn away from him and drink my water. After we finished our bottles we made our way back out to the dance floor.

A human man moved over, trying to dance with me and I laughed at the comparison of his muscled body next to Sean's. If the man had done steroids he might have been as big as Sean, but usually only hardcore bodybuilders looked close to how werewolf males looked. Luckily the females weren't so muscular, but we had our fair amount of muscle. Sean moved between the human and me and I could see the tension in his shoulders. Dominants didn't like someone coming between them and a female.

The man took the hint and walked away. I smiled at Sean and kissed his cheek for not ripping the man's throat out. The song changed to a fast beat and Sean and I easily matched its tempo. A female human walked over and started dancing with Sean. I fought my urge to snarl and decided to test Sean. I kept dancing, ignoring the silicone enhanced woman, and Sean raised his eyebrow at me. He subtly moved around to dance behind me, but the woman wasn't giving up that easily. She started dancing with me, and then slowly made her way to dance next to Sean. I felt the air whoosh out of his lungs as he sighed. He moved to face me and frowned, trying to convey his irritation.

I laughed and moved closer to him so that there was no space between us, successfully discouraging the woman. He had been keeping his hands to his sides, but I could see the golden specks forming in his eyes. Apparently, I was tripping all of the right switches, but that wasn't necessarily a good thing for me. I stepped back from him as I smelled his wolf and lowered my hand, ready to draw the knife if he tried to attack me.

He inhaled deeply and I watched in amazement as the gold faded along with the smell of his wolf. I pointed towards the exit and he nodded, taking my hand gently again as we maneu-vered through the crowded room.

We stood outside, and stood silently for a moment, letting our eardrums relax and inhaling the night air. I looked up at Sean's happy face and asked, "How did you do that?"

He frowned. "Do what?"

I started walking so I would have something to do besides stare at him. "Your wolf woke up. I could smell him and see the gold in your eyes, and you stopped it. I've never seen a male who was able to do that."

Sean shook his head sadly. "You really need to hang out with some new males."

I continued walking, not wanting to dance anymore and truly needing to go to bed soon.

We stopped in front of my house and Sean asked softly, "Did I hold up to our deal?"

The night had been fun and I really had enjoyed myself. True to his word he hadn't tried anything and I hadn't needed the knife strapped to my leg. A few moments of pain were worth getting to know him, I supposed. "Sure, come in." As soon as I said the words little warning lights blazed in my head. I was letting a dominant male wolf into my house. I forced myself to relax and prayed that Sean was as good of a guy as I thought he was.

He followed me into the house and then sat down on the couch. I locked the door back up before sitting in the recliner across from him. "What do you want me to tell you?"

He frowned for a moment than asked, "Start with being bitten and then tell me about your pack and why you broke your ties with them."

I pulled my legs up and wrapped my arms around them. I knew it looked juvenile, but I needed some type of comfort while I discussed my story.

"I was eighteen, living in Miami, and dating Jeff. He seemed like a good guy, you know opening doors for me, never using foul language if I was there. He was different than any other man I'd been with because he had an allure of danger, but he was always sweet to me. After being together for a few months he told me that he wanted to take our relationship to the next level. I assumed he meant sex, but he ripped off his clothes and changed. I was too scared to move, and just stood there like an idiot as he bit my arm. I woke up three days later in a cage with silver bars. I tried to get out, but they wouldn't let me, and the silver burned. The full moon was only two days later and I changed in the cage for the first time. It was so painful and the cage was so small..." I stopped for a moment as I shuddered at the memory of that wicked cage.

"Eventually they let me out and that's when Jeff discovered that I didn't smell right to him anymore. He was easily angered, which I hadn't noticed before, and anytime I messed up, he hit me. I tried to run away, but they always found me. All of the males in the pack had trouble controlling their wolves and with a female now in the group, it brought more tension and more fights. If Jeff hadn't been as dominant as he was, and beta, he would have been killed by the members of the pack that challenged him. One night the males were especially agitated and decided that to release their anger it would be fun to..." A sob tried to escape, but I held it in, squeezing my eyes shut.

Sean moved across the living room and wiped the tears from my face. "Shh... I'm sorry. You don't have to—"

I shook my head and opened my eyes. "I need to finish." He moved back to his seat and I exhaled. "There were only five males home that night, but the rape didn't stop. Every night they found a reason to beat and then rape me. John, the alpha, never joined in, but he would watch and I could smell his arousal. He *never* stopped them. He never used the soothing magic that you have. They kept me locked in the cage so I wouldn't run, but one night I convinced one of the dumber members to let me out so I could *please* him. He didn't notice the metal pipe sitting inside my cage, and when he opened the door I knocked him out. I ran for three days straight, but the alpha was calling me back to him. I fought it as hard as I could, but against my will I started heading back. That's when I broke my pack ties and came out here."

I looked up slowly, because I could feel Sean's anger like hot rain scalding my skin. His eyes were perfect golden wolf's eyes as he stared at me. He stood up very slowly and walked out of the house.

I guess he didn't want a used female.

I walked to my bedroom and changed into a pair of sweats and a t-shirt before walking back out to the living room and putting the flowers he had given me in a vase with water. No one had ever given me flowers before.

The ice cream was calling my name, so I opened the freezer and pulled it out. Sean opened the front door and walked inside, his eyes back to hazel, but I could still smell his anger. He sat down on one of the stools at the counter and took a deep cleansing breath. "Thank you for telling me."

I kept my eyes down so as not to challenge him and nodded. "It was our deal."

He held out his hand and I set a piece of the ice cream in it. He popped it in his mouth and moaned. "This is good. What is this?"

I laughed. "Chocolate dipped vanilla ice cream."

He plucked one out of the container. "I've got to remember to buy some of these."

I handed him one more and then closed the lid, and put it inside the freezer. He was suddenly standing behind me, and I froze. My heart beat picked up and I waited for the hit that always came.

I whispered, "I'm sorry. I didn't know you wanted more."

He inhaled and then stepped back. "I didn't mean to frighten you. I just…I'm sorry." He stepped back farther and I stared at him with wide eyes. He had apologized again and actually meant it. No males ever apologized.

He moved forward slowly and wrapped his arms around my shoulders, hugging me. "I just wanted to do this."

His body was hot like werewolves were, and it felt good to be pressed against him. He hugged me against his chest and a soothing wind of magic wrapped around me. I relaxed against him and he tilted my chin up so that I was looking into his blue and brown eyes. "I will never harm you. You do not have to do anything with me. If you want me to stop, tell me. If you want me to leave, tell me. Okay?"

I nodded and stood on tiptoe to kiss him on the lips. His lips were gentle and uncertain as he kissed me back, but just as soft as I had imagined. I stepped back from him and turned away. "I understand if you don't want to see me anymore." My voice cracked and I wished it hadn't. I barely knew him and yet I was already fond of him. My wolf already wanted to run with his again.

He turned me back around and looked over my face. "Why wouldn't I want to see you anymore?"

Traitorous tears leaked out of my eyes before I could stop them. "Because I'm damaged," I whispered

He shook his head. "What happened wasn't your fault. What they did to you was not anything you could have prevented. You may be damaged, but I can repair you, if you'll let me." He wiped the tears from my eyes and kissed me softly on the lips. He whispered, "I can also break the mate bond you're still stuck with, if you want me to."

I sniffed and turned away to grab a paper towel to blow my nose. He waited patiently as I recomposed myself. "I don't want to see your alpha," I said quietly. Sean nodded, but didn't say anything. "And I would greatly appreciate it if you could break the mate bond. I don't ever want to go back to Jeff again, not after what he put me through."

"Okay, it's easy and won't hurt you at all."

"Can we do it another day? I'm really tired," I whispered.

He stepped back from me and smiled. "Of course."

I followed him, mouth slightly agape, as he headed towards the front door and opened it.

He bent down and kissed my cheek softly. "Thank you, Rose. I hope I can see you again soon."

"Thank you for tonight," I whispered.

He smiled happily at me and walked to his car. I shut the door and sagged against it as a smile split my face. He was amazing.

Chapter 5

I called into work the next day and after explaining I'd been up all night with Mr. Wright, Richard had been more than happy to let me off.

I hadn't expected our date to go as well as it had. I really hadn't expected him to want to see me again after learning what had happened and understanding how broken I was. Honestly, I had expected him to force me to let him stay the night, but he had behaved like a perfect gentleman. Was it just a trick? Or was he really just nice? I knew he was right about every person being different, but was it true of male werewolves? Could it be because he was a born wolf instead of a bitten wolf?

I contemplated what I should do and what I thought of him as I ran around the park that morning. I didn't usually run in the mornings, but our date had kept me out and I needed to burn off energy. As I walked back to my house, my cell phone rang.

"Hello?" I answered.

"Hi," Sean said cheerfully. "What are you up to?"

"Just out for a jog," I said nonchalantly. "You?"

"Well I was hoping we could meet for lunch?"

My instant reaction was no, but that wasn't really fair to him since he had been incredibly good to me last night. I chewed on my lip as I thought about it. Maybe I should test him? "I'm not really hungry right now," I lied. "Maybe another time."

I knew he could sense I was lying and honestly, I wanted to see what his reaction to being turned down was. Jeff would never have allowed me to reject him.

"Okay," he said, sounding somewhat disappointed. "Well, I guess I'll let you get back to your jog then."

"Okay. Bye." I hung up the phone and stared at it in disbelief. He'd taken the rejection well, hadn't gotten angry or even tried to persuade me. Was this guy for real? I turned back around and jogged around the park six more times to release the nervous energy thrumming through me. If he was for real, I might actually be able to spend time with a wolf again! A playmate sounded like heaven.

As I ate my ice cream on my couch that afternoon, I decided to do something nice and to further pursue my tests on him.

"Hello?" he answered after the second ring.

"Hey, it's Rose."

"Hey, Rose," he said happily.

"I was wondering if you would be up to dinner and a movie?" I asked, trying my hardest to calm my racing heart and not sound as nervous as I felt.

"That sounds great," he said sounding genuinely pleased. "Where would you like to eat?"

"I can eat anywhere, so why don't you pick?" I suggested. Truthfully, I couldn't ever make up my mind about where I wanted to go so it was easier if he just picked.

"How about Milton's Steakhouse?"

My mouth watered at the name like I'd heard Pavlov's bell. "That sounds great."

"I'll pick you up at five, okay?"

"Okay," I said. We hung up and I realized I was smiling. I looked at the clock, shocked to see it was already three and rushed to shower and get ready. Since tonight was a relaxed date, I opted for jeans and a t-shirt. He had to see me as I truly was and I wasn't a girl who wore nice clothes every night. I had been when I was in college, but not after everything that had happened to me.

I was pacing in the living room when I heard his car pull up to the curb. I started to move towards the door, but held myself back and waited for him to knock. Even though I heard every movement he made, I still jumped when he knocked on the door. I took two deep breaths, and then opened the door.

"Hello," he said with a bright smile on his face.

He looked incredibly hot in a tight-fitting black t-shirt and blue jeans. I smiled back at him and asked, "How are you tonight?"

He stepped back to allow me room on the porch without me feeling crowded. "I'm in a very good mood now," he said as he backed down the steps.

I locked the door and followed him. "Were you having a bad day?" I asked.

He shrugged. "I got rejected for a lunch date and thought I might have messed up."

"So, you were upset you got rejected?" I asked, watching his body and listening for his reaction.

"I was sad I was rejected, but more upset that I might have messed things up with the girl," he answered honestly as he held open the passenger door for me.

I waited until he was inside the car before asking, "Would that be so bad?"

He was silent a moment and I glanced over to see what he

was doing. His nostrils were flaring and he was looking at me out of the corners of his eyes. I almost laughed because I realized he was trying to figure out my mood. He parked the car and said, "It would have made me very sad because even though I barely know the girl, I really like her. She's beautiful and smart and best of all she knows what I am." My shock must have been apparent because he smiled and whispered, "Hopefully I don't ruin this date or scare her away."

I smiled back at him and said, "I'm sure any woman would be lucky to have you."

He shrugged. "If you say so."

We stepped out of the car and went into the steakhouse, immediately getting a reserved table. I didn't want to cost him too much so I was prepared to order a ten-ounce steak, but when the waiter came he ordered for both of us, getting me their largest twenty-ounce steak. "You didn't have to get me that big of a steak," I said.

He sipped from his water glass and then said, "I'm not a cheap jerk. Besides, I know you could truly eat two of the twenty-ounce steaks before even feeling remotely satisfied. Please don't feel like you need to save me money or like you can't order what you truly want. If you want three steaks and two desserts then feel free to order it."

"I wouldn't do that," I said seriously. "Besides, this date was my idea."

He shrugged. "It's more like the rain check from my lunch date."

"Why are you really interested in me? Do you just want to force me to join your pack?"

He reached for my hand on top of the table and I jerked it back quickly, afraid I'd made him mad and he was going to hurt me somehow. He set his hand on the table, palm up and whispered, "I would never force you to do anything. I'm interested in you because you're beautiful and sweet and I truly want to get to know you better. If we dated another year and you still didn't want to join my pack, I wouldn't force you."

We both knew that his alpha would, though. It wasn't allowed to be a lone wolf, especially when you were living within a pack's territory.

"I want to see the real you," I whispered to him. "Not this guy you're pretending to be."

He pulled his hand back and shook his head sadly. "I'm not pretending to be anything. What you see is what you get with me."

"If that were true these humans would be running away in terror," I said.

He rolled his eyes. "You know what I am. You've seen me in wolf form."

"And what are you like when you get mad?" I asked softly.

"I'm me, but angry. I still have morals, which include not hurting humans if possible, and never hurting females unless my life is in danger. What are you like when you're angry?"

"A bitch," I said with a smirk.

He laughed and whispered, "Rose, I swear that I am not like the wolves you've met. I am not cruel or psychotic. I wish you would believe me and I wish there was someway for me to prove it to you."

There was a way, but I was too afraid of him hurting me to allow it.

"Here you go," The waiter said as he set our food down for us.

We ate our dinner without speaking, but my mind was whirling a mile a minute. There had to be some way for me to test him. Some way for me to make him reveal his true nature. He couldn't be as perfect as he seemed. There had to be a flaw.

"Would you like dessert?" he asked.

I shook my head. "Not here, thank you. I might like some candy at the movies."

He paid the bill and we walked back to his car. The night was cool and perfect, but strange scents continued to waft past my nose. I was almost to the car when someone screamed and charged at me from behind. I spun around, ready to protect myself, but Sean was already standing between me and the man who had tried to attack me. The man was human, obviously strung out on drugs, and holding a knife.

"Back off," Sean said angrily. The anger in his voice made me cringe and step away from him and into the side of the car.

"If you don't want to get hurt, pretty boy, just give me your money," the human said.

"If you want to live, I suggest you turn and walk away," Sean replied.

"You asked for it!" the human yelled and then charged forward, slashing the knife.

Sean sidestepped the swings easily, and then grabbed the man's hand and broke his wrist. The man cried out in pain and backed away. "Walk away," Sean said in a calm voice.

The man turned and ran in the opposite direction. I dug my feet into the ground and hugged myself to keep from chasing after the man. It was always so much fun when prey ran. I looked at Sean and was shocked to see that he had turned around and was facing me. I expected his eyes to be golden or his face to be angry, but he looked as calm as he had when we'd left the restaurant.

"Are you alright?" he asked.

I looked down and saw the knife now in his hand and a growl slipped through my teeth.

He whispered, "Easy, Rose. I'm just going to put it in the trash can so no one runs over it out here in the parking lot. Watch." I kept my eyes on him, and turned my body with his as he walked in a wide arc around me to the trashcan by the street and put the knife inside it. He held up his hands, showing that they were empty. "See, all gone."

I exhaled and clenched my eyes against the memories of knives being used against me. "I'm sorry."

"Are you alright?" he asked again.

I nodded and opened my eyes. "Yes."

He stood just in front of me and whispered, "Do you want to continue our date or would you like to go home?"

I was shocked that he would even consider ending the date. I knew I needed to calm down before I blew this. "No, I'm alright. We better hurry if we want to get good seats, though." I smiled at him and climbed in to the car.

He climbed in and whispered, "You don't have to do this if you don't want to. I won't get mad at you if you tell me you want to go home."

I had heard that before and received bruises for it, but for some reason I felt like he was being truly honest. "I don't want to go home," I told him. "I want to go the movies with you."

He smiled. "Good." It didn't take us as long as I'd thought because we lucked into a parking spot near the front. He paid for our tickets and then for our snacks during the movie, which included hot dogs for each of us, popcorn, soda, and candy. When I was a human I would have had to go running two hours that day to make up for eating that much. Sometimes it was good to be a werewolf.

I chose seats in the very center of the movie theater so that we were surrounded by humans and I could watch how he reacted. Personally, I didn't like humans, but having been a human before being turned made me more tolerable of them. He had chosen a comedy movie with one of my favorite actors in it, and I settled in, ready to enjoy the movie. The humans filed in, searching for friends and looking for decent seats.

"Do you *like* your job?" he asked me while I was people watching.

"It's an okay job. Pretty easy and the pay is okay."

"Is there something you would rather do?" he asked as he munched on pieces of popcorn.

"I used to want to be a dancer, but now I feel like it would be cheating," I told him honestly. I hadn't ever told anyone that, but I knew it was because he made me feel so at ease. Even though I was prepared for him to try to attack me, I felt calm and relaxed. A group of women who were obviously out on a girl's night spotted Sean and started making their way down the row in front of us. I bent down to pick up my ticket stub, which had *accidentally* fallen from my hand and watched his reaction to the women in front of us.

"Why can't you join a dance troupe and then it won't matter if you're better because you're making the same as everyone else during shows?" he asked as he looked down at me, completely ignoring the women.

I sat up and had to flip my hair back, which wafted my scent towards him. "I don't know. I'd still be worried about the monthly problem I have to take a week of vacation for getting in the way."

His nostrils flared and golden sparks danced within his eyes. He moved closer to me and whispered, "You smell incredibly good."

For the first time in years I didn't shudder when a man complimented me. For the first time, I smiled back. "Thank you." The lights dimmed and I relaxed back into my seat as the previews started.

The movie was hilarious and as we walked to his car I realized that he still hadn't shown any signs of putting on an act. Could I have really lucked into finding a great guy? A werewolf who respected females?

I knew there was one last test I needed to do in order to make him fully prove his intentions and I decided I had to do it, even if he did end up hurting me. He dropped me off at home and walked me to the door, but only kissed my cheek before turning around and leaving. Even when I was a human, men would push the issue of coming inside and trying to get some action. Was he not pushing me because of my past? Whatever the reason, it made me like him even more and I made the decision to call him tomorrow to come over.

Chapter 6

Work seemed to take twice as long that next day, but luckily Richard kept me busy with letters and pleadings and meetings so that my mind was busy and I didn't have much time to think about Sean.

At lunch, I had text messaged him and he had agreed to come to my house for dinner. I didn't have much at the house, but I planned to use some of the bonus money I had received and buy food just for tonight.

It had been so long since I'd had a man over and cooked for him, that I felt on edge. I rushed through the grocery store, grabbing everything I needed for the night, and rushed back home. There wasn't much time before he was supposed to come, but I did as much as I could and had the food halfway done when I heard his car pull up to the curb. I checked my appearance, and then set the small two-seater table I had with plates and silverware.

He knocked on the door and I called, "It's open."

He opened the door and inhaled with a wide smile on his face. "It smells delicious in here."

I smiled back and stirred the pasta that was now simmering. "It should be ready in a minute."

He sat down on one of the bar stools and asked, "How was work?"

"Busy, but that's good sometimes. How was your day?" I asked.

He watched me rush around the kitchen and shrugged. "It was okay, but I couldn't stop thinking about you all day."

I smiled and turned off the burners. "Okay, dinner is done. If you grab your plate you can come serve yourself."

He took both of our plates off the table and handed me mine. "It looks great, Rose. Thank you."

I moved out of the kitchen so that I wasn't trapped in the corner while he made his plate and watched him. My heart was beating faster than normal as I thought about my plan for that night and I knew he could hear my heart, but nothing I did calmed it. He sat down at the table with his full plate and I filled mine up quickly so as not to keep him waiting.

He stabbed a piece of chicken and pasta and put it into his mouth, chewing slowly. I watched in anticipation, waiting to see if it tasted good or if he disliked it. He finished it and smiled. "It's delicious!"

I exhaled and started eating with him. "Thank you. I was worried you might not like it. I haven't cooked for another person in years."

"It's really great," he said honestly.

We ate in silence and then I stood and took his empty plate to the sink. "Would you like dessert now, or later?" I asked him.

He laughed softly. "You know I could eat more now, so whatever you want."

I pulled out the cherry cheesecake I had made and cut a big slice for him, putting it on a small dessert plate. "Here you go. I made it myself."

He took the cheesecake and whistled. "Wow, this is

amazing."

"It's the only thing I know how to bake," I admitted.

He took a bite and moaned. "Well you do it really well."

I laughed and cut a slice for myself, but ate bites slowly as I put away the leftovers and started the dishes. Sean brought me his dessert plate and kissed my cheek. "Thank you for dinner."

"You're welcome." I finished putting the food away and asked, "Would you like to watch some television or a movie?"

He smiled and nodded. "Yeah."

We sat down on the couch and I turned on the television. He put his arm around my shoulders and I didn't feel fear or flinch away from him. Was I being dumb in letting my guard down? We watched TV for a couple hours, but my eyes were starting to droop and he noticed.

"You seem tired," he whispered as he stroked my hair. "Maybe I should go?"

He stood and I grabbed his hand, pulling at what little courage I had and asked, "Would you mind staying the night with me?"

He pulled me up off the couch and then slowly picked me up in his arms so as not to startle me. "I'd like nothing better." He carried me to the bedroom, turning off lights and locking the front door on the way. He took his shirt and shoes off and climbed into bed beside me. Warning bells rang and I quickly tamped them down. He had promised he would never hurt me and I had heard the truth in his words. One night wouldn't mean anything and it would help me see what his true intentions were.

He wrapped his arms around me and whispered, "I'll protect you. No one will harm you ever again. And I'll break your bond while you're sleeping. Jeff will no longer have any control over you and you will be your own wolf." His reassuring words and his presence brought sleep over me faster than it ever had before.

Chapter 7

I woke up the next morning alone in my bed. I walked out to the living room, smiling to know that Sean had stayed true to his word and not tried anything even though we had been sleeping in the same bed together and hehad broken the mate bond I had had with Jeff.

Sean smiled at me from the kitchen where he was cooking eggs, bacon, and pancakes. "Hey, sleepy."

I rubbed my eyes and frowned. "What time is it?"

He pointed to the clock hanging on my wall as if he lived here instead of me. "Ten in the morning."

I stared at the clock's hands in shock. I hadn't slept in this late since before I was bitten. "I'm so sorry. You should have woken me."

I started to come into the kitchen and he shook his head. "Go get dressed and I will finish breakfast."

I opened my mouth to object, but he ignored me, flipping over a pancake. I quickly went through my morning routine and changed into a pair of jeans and a t-shirt. When I came back out to the living room, two plates of fully prepared food sat on the counter in front of the stools. He had even poured two glasses of milk. I frowned. "I didn't have milk."

He smiled. "I made a quick trip to the store while you were sleeping."

I walked to the fridge and my mouth dropped open in disbelief at the amount of food stuffed inside it. I opened the freezer and it was equally full. I quickly opened all of my cupboards. I felt dizzy. "How much did you spend?"

He shook his head not willing to answer so I grabbed my purse and pulled out two one hundred dollar bills from my bonus money and held them out to him. "Here."

He shook his head and held up his hands. "I don't want your money."

"This is your money. You paid for the food."

He smiled and kissed my cheek. "Consider it a gift."

He's stubborn. I'll just have to slip it in his pockets at some point. I set the money on the coffee table and walked to sit on one of the stools. He sat down beside me and started eating. He was in such a good mood that I didn't want to spoil it so I ate with him. I finished my plate of ten pancakes, five pieces of bacon, and five eggs and took his empty plate with mine to the sink. He gently pushed me to the side away from the sink and started doing the dishes.

"Sean, this is my house and I asked you to stay. You shouldn't have cooked breakfast for me, and you sure as hell shouldn't do the dishes, too. You especially shouldn't be doing anything for me since you also broke my mate bond."

He shrugged. "I'm already doing them, so you might as well go sit down and relax. And you don't owe me anything for breaking your old mate bond. I enjoyed breaking it." I opened my mouth to argue and he said, "I'm almost done."

I sighed and walked to the couch. It was nice to have someone looking after me, but it was wrong that a dominant was doing things for me. He finished the dishes and sat down beside me on the couch to watch TV. We watched the television in silence, me in complete bliss. He took me out for lunch and then we walked through the park. He hadn't spoken much and I was starting to get worried that I had upset him somehow.

"Are you upset about something?" I asked him.

He looked at me with a frown. "No, why would you think that?"

"You've been awfully quiet."

"Sorry, I've just been thinking."

"About?"

"Will you go on a trip with me this weekend?"

A weekend trip?

"Where?"

"To Tahoe," he said. "I have a cabin up there."

I chewed on my lip nervously. In the city, he would be more likely to get caught if he hurt me, but in the mountains, he could dispose of my body without anyone finding or knowing. I didn't really think Sean would do that, but I hadn't known him very long.

"I don't know."

"We could spend an entire weekend away from the city and humans, unless you wanted to go to the casinos. We could spend it as wolves or in human form. We could just enjoy each other and not think about packs or anything else. It would just be the two of us."

It did sound amazing.

"Okay," I said finally in a soft voice, shocked I had even said it.

He smiled happily and hugged me tightly. "You won't regret it, I promise."

"When would we leave?"

"Friday night."

That was tomorrow.

When we got back to my house he said he needed to go take care of some stuff for the trip.

I snatched the cash off the table before he could see me and walked him to the door. "Thank you for last night and the food this morning."

He hugged me against him and rubbed his cheek against mine.

Possessive, much?

"Can I come back tonight?"

I should have said no, but I wanted to see him again. "Sure." He kissed me lightly on the lips and I shoved the money in his back pocket before pushing him gently out of the door.

He pulled the money out of his pocket and frowned at me.

I waved. "See you tonight."

I closed the door and heard him laughing as he walked away.

I looked through my clothes and spent the entire evening picking out clothes to take on the trip with me. I was actually looking forward to the trip.

Work was unbearable the next day and Richard pressured me constantly to get details about Sean and me, but I continued to ignore him. At the end of the day I ran out of the office and to my house as fast as I could, so I could get the last few items I needed ready.

Sean knocked on the door a few minutes after six and I yelled for him to come inside. I zipped up my bag and turned around to find a single red rose in front of me. I took it from him and he kissed my cheek.

"Are you ready?" he asked.

I set the flower on my dresser and nodded. "Yeah." Part of me knew it came out as a lie, since I was incredibly nervous, but I didn't want to ruin the weekend before it had started.

He took my bag and headed out to his car. "Well let's get going!"

I locked the house up and slid into the passenger seat of his truck. "I'm surprised you have a beat up looking truck like this," I admitted.

He laughed. "It's the perfect vehicle for going off road. A nice truck would just get dirty and banged up anyways."

"Was your alpha okay with us going?" I asked softly.

"Of course. I'm an adult, I don't have to get his permission to go on dates."

"Mmhm."

He started the truck and then reached over, resting his hand palm up on my leg. I slid my hand into his and felt a weird tingling in my head as we held hands. I had had it since he broke my mate bond. Maybe it was a side effect from it. I really didn't care. I was thrilled to no longer be tied to that pack in any way.

I turned the radio on low and relaxed in the seat as he drove. "How was work?" I asked him.

"Fine, I set up a Tahiti honeymoon package for a couple getting married at the end of the year."

"I've always wanted to go outside the country," I admitted.

"Why haven't you?"

"I don't have any of my birth certificates anymore, so I can't get a passport."

"You can order a birth certificate," he advised me. "It is really simple. I could help you if you wanted me to."

"Maybe," I said.

"So, you haven't mentioned your family," he commented.

"Both my parents are dead," I said softly. The sadness from their deaths was still strong, especially since I had been the cause.

"I'm sorry, Rose. What happened?"

"The pack killed them," I admitted.

His hand tightened around mine, but he controlled his anger enough that I didn't sense it. "Why?"

"They did it after the third time I ran away."

"I hope I get to meet these guys," he growled.

"I don't," I whispered in fear. I never wanted to see them again and I really didn't want them to hurt Sean.

He stroked his thumb across my hand as he held it. "Don't worry about me, I'm a decent fighter."

"Sean, if they hurt you, I could never forgive myself."

"Easy, Rose. I won't get hurt by these idiots and even if I did, it wouldn't be your fault. Let's forget about it, okay."

I couldn't forget about it. The thought that Jeff might find me and hurt Sean had already crossed my mind many times. Maybe it would be smarter to isolate myself so that no one could get hurt.

"Rose, you're perfectly safe with me. Nothing bad is going to happen. Ok?"

I took a deep breath and blew it out slowly. "What about your family?" I asked him.

"My dad and I aren't on good terms at the moment. My mom died a long time ago."

"I'm sorry."

He shrugged. "I was too young to know my mom and my dad isn't easy to get along with, anyways."

"Have you always been in this pack?" I asked.

He nodded. "Born and raised."

"Why don't you have a mate?"

"I told you, there aren't many free females around."

"Yeah, but there are some, and you're hot."

He smirked. "Most of the females who are free are a bit crazy and not my type."

"All females are crazy."

He laughed. "No comment."

I turned and looked at him as he drove. Why me? I scooted

closer to him since the seat was a bench seat and leaned my head on his shoulder. Even if things didn't work out between Sean and me, I should enjoy it while it was happening. He turned and kissed the top of my head while still watching the road.

He released my hand and moved his arm so that it was wrapped around my shoulders. I relaxed against him and said, "I could get used to this."

"Me too," he whispered and rubbed my shoulder.

"What do you do for fun?" I asked him since I had been quiet for far too long.

"I take trips a lot. I try to see as much of the world as possible. I go to the beach a lot and surf."

"You know how to surf?"

"Yeah."

"I've always wanted to learn to surf."

"I'll have to teach you then."

"I don't even own a bathing suit anymore," I whispered to myself.

"Why not?"

Crap, I hadn't meant to say that out loud.

"Uh, I don't really wear revealing clothes much anymore."

He rubbed my shoulder again and said, "Well you are welcome to wear whatever you want around me."

"I'm sure you wouldn't mind me wearing revealing clothes," I said with a laugh.

"Hm," he mumbled.

"Have you ever had a mate before?" I asked him softly.

He shook his head. "No."

"Does it bother you that I have?"

He glanced at me and then looked back at the road. "Not at all. Your past is your past, and it's what shaped you into the person you are, who I really like."

There was a lie in there somewhere.

"You're lying," I whispered.

He sighed. "It bothers me that those men took advantage of you. It doesn't make me think less of you, but I don't like thinking about them hurting you."

"If I could take it back—"

"I meant what I said about it shaping you into who you are. And I meant what I said about really liking you. I like who you are now and I don't care what you did in your past and just want to make your future one that you will enjoy."

"You seem certain that you will want to stay with me for there to be a future."

"Well, you're beautiful, smart, sweet, and fun to spend time with. My wolf and yours get along great and so far, I haven't seen a reason yet why I wouldn't want to spend more time with you."

He pulled off the freeway and onto a road that led to a small cabin right next to the lake.

"I'm broken," I whispered.

He turned the truck off and turned to face me, putting a hand underneath my chin and said, "I can help you heal."

"How do you know? Why would you want to help me?"

"You know why," he whispered as he stared into my eyes. He leaned forward and kissed me deeply. I melted into him and kissed him back. He was the first man I had kissed since Jeff, and for the first time, I wasn't afraid. He pulled back and leaned his forehead against mine. "Will you let me help you?"

"What do I have to do?"

"Just enjoy being with me. Forget about your past and focus on our now. Can you do that?"

I nodded and rubbed my face against his. "Yes."

He beamed happily and crushed me against him in a tight hug. "Come on, let's get everything put away so we can go play."

We spent the rest of the night in wolf form and fell asleep on the rug in front of the fireplace curled around each other.

When we arrived back from our trip, we sat on the couch together watching shows and relaxing, cuddled together.

Sean's cell phone rang, ending the pleasant mood a few minutes later. "Sean," he answered quickly.

Werewolves had very good hearing, and I could hear the person on the other end of the phone. He was older with a deep voice that I recognized, but couldn't place. "Where are you?"

Sean adjusted his butt on the couch. "With a friend."

The man sighed softly. "You're with her again, aren't you?" Sean didn't answer, which was answer enough. "I won't order you to bring her in. If she's not ready, then I'll wait for her. But, she needs to come see me before the next full moon. I don't want another incident like last moon happening again."

Sean nodded. "I understand."

The man laughed softly. "You're as stubborn as your father was. I need to speak with you. Come back to the hall."

Sean sighed and closed his phone. "I need to go."

He kissed me goodbye, and I watched him go.

I leaned against the door long after he was gone, and realized I was smiling. He had made me smile yet again.

The farther away he got though, the more my fear returned.

What was I doing? I'd heard his alpha. He wanted me to come in, but I couldn't. I couldn't go back! My cell phone rang from inside my room and I ran to answer it. "Hello?"

Richard asked, "What happened? How come you didn't come in to work?"

I groaned. "I'm sorry Richard. We were out late last night and he didn't wake me up."

"He stayed the night?"

I groaned again. "Yes, but nothing happened."

"He stayed the night and nothing happened? What the hell is wrong with you? Well I guess you wouldn't want to come off easy, but still... Don't come in today, nothing's happening. Are you going to see him again?"

I wanted to say no, that I was leaving, but I couldn't just run from Sean. "Yes, tonight."

Richard giggled excitedly. "Okay, don't come in to work tomorrow then, but call me."

"Okay, bye." I hung up before he could talk anymore. What a girl Richard was! I busied myself cleaning the house and then reorganized the cabinets of food. By the time I had the cabinets, fridge, and freezer organized, it was dark outside. I hopped into the shower and washed everything, but my face, leaving Sean's scent on my cheek. I redressed, packed a suitcase, and started taking out boxed pasta and chicken when someone knocked on my door. I walked cautiously towards the door and inhaled a few feet away.

Sean.

I opened the door and he smiled at me. "Hey."

I stepped away from the door to let him in. "Hi." I moved away from him and back to the kitchen before he could hug me. I would make him food then tell him I was leaving. That seemed the easiest way.

I pulled out pots and pans and Sean sat down on a stool watching me.

He inhaled then frowned. "What's wrong?"

I stopped moving and looked at him. "What do you mean?"

He folded his arms across his chest. "You're nervous and afraid."

I swallowed. Stupid werewolf senses. I couldn't lie to him, but I could fib a little. "I have something I need to talk to you about and I'm worried how you'll react."

His eyes widened and he unfolded his arms. "Okay."

I shook my head. "Let me make food first."

He stood and walked around the room. I didn't have any pictures or movies, so he didn't really have much to look at. He looked at my boring black couch, my plain wall clock, my old brown recliner, and then he looked into my bedroom door. His whole body tensed and I could smell his nervousness from the kitchen. He looked back at me. "Why is there a suitcase on your bed?"

Shit. I thought I'd put it under the bed.

I ignored him and kept preparing the food.

He sat down on the stool again and watched me silently. *Why was he nervous? I'm the one running away again.* I turned on the radio while the food was simmering and Sean walked to stand behind me. He wrapped his arms around me and hugged me against him. "You're too wound up. Relax." His magic enveloped me, now familiar with the feel of it and my body relaxed against him. He began swaying and I let him lead me into a slow dance out of the kitchen and into the living room. He turned me around to face him and kissed my lips softly. "I think dinner's burning."

I jumped away from him and ran back into the kitchen, turning off the stove. I moved the pots to different burners and then turned to face the wall. Why did he make me feel like this? Why was I letting myself get so close to him? I hit my head against the wall and Sean rushed over, turning me around. He stared at my face in shock and hugged me. "What's wrong? What did I do? Why are you crying?"

Crying? I touched my face and felt the wetness. I pulled away from him and wiped at my eyes before pulling plates down.

He was upset now and paced across the living room.

I filled up our plates and set them on the counter with glasses of water. We ate our food in silence, and then I washed the dishes. He started pacing again as soon as I'd taken his plate. He stopped in mid-stride and asked, "Where are you going?"

I stopped washing dishes, and turned to him. "I need to leave. I can't go see your alpha because he'll send me back. You have to understand that I can't go back."

He shook his head. "He wouldn't send you back."

"Yes, he will. I'm sorry, but I can't stay here. I heard him tell you that I have to come to him before the next moon. *I have to leave.*"

He stopped pacing and pulled me against him, kissing me fiercely. I wanted to pull away to say no, but my hands found their way up to his neck and I was kissing him back. He kissed his way down my jaw and to my neck and licked across my pulse. I shivered against him, surprised that my wolf senses weren't trying to warn me that he could hurt me. He ran his hand up my back and whispered, "Don't leave me."

I sniffed as I fought not to cry at the pain he was experiencing. "I can't stay here. They'll find me. It's nothing to do with you. You've been great to me. Better than anyone's ever treated me before."

He rubbed his face against mine and whined softly. "Stay with me. I'll protect you. I won't let them send you back."

I shook my head and dropped my hands, which had somehow made their way to his chest. "If your alpha tells you to send me away, you'll have to do it."

He shook his head. "I'll run with you. Let me come with you and we'll run away together."

I stepped back and frowned. "You can't leave your pack."

He inhaled and I could see how confused he was. "Just talk to my alpha. If he says he wants to send you back, then I'll help you escape. I may not be able to do it personally, but I have human contacts that can help you. Please at least talk to my alpha. Please. I don't want to lose you."

Would talking to his alpha hurt? Surely, he wouldn't send me back to Jeff and the other bastards in John's pack.

I didn't want to leave Sean. The thought of leaving him made my heart hurt. It was too soon for me to feel this way and yet I was. I looked up into Sean's pleading eyes and whispered, "I'll go meet with him, but if he tries to send me back, you have to promise to help me run."

Sean picked me up and spun me around. "You won't regret this. I promise I'll help if he tries to send you back."

I kissed his cheek and he set me down. "Did you put some type of spell on me?" I asked quietly.

He frowned down at me. "What? No? Why do you think I put a spell on you?"

I blushed. "I've just never felt so strongly for someone I barely know."

He smiled. "Your wolf approves of mine and mine of yours. That's all they need to know. Come on, let's go."

I nodded and let him lead me out of the house. I locked up the door and then we started walking down the street. He picked my hand up holding it as we walked. I looked up at his face and saw how happy this decision had made him. I just hoped his alpha didn't try to send me away. He opened the door to an expensive Lexus a few blocks from my house and smiled at me. "The pack lives a few miles outside of the city. Promise I won't kill you with my driving."

I climbed into the car and ran my hand along the dashboard. "Is this yours?" I asked as he climbed in the driver's seat. He had driven different cars every time we had gone out.

He nodded. "This is one of my cars. I have three." I stared at him and he laughed. "I told you that the pack helps each other out." He held my hand again as we drove and I relaxed against the seat. He turned on the radio and we listened to hard rock music. I closed my eyes and was almost asleep when Sean cleared his throat. "We're here."

I opened my eyes and looked at the mansion we were stopped in front of. "This is the pack's house?"

He nodded.

I whistled. "You guys must blackmail a lot of people."

He shook his head. "We don't blackmail anyone." I didn't want to argue even though I had smelled his lie, so I smiled and climbed out of the car. Two males in pants and no shirts stood at the front door staring down at us. Sean laced his fingers through mine and whispered, "Don't be scared. They won't hurt you."

I stepped a little closer to him as we walked up the stairs. Sean placed his fist over his heart and bowed to the males. "Greetings Brothers."

The two males mimicked him and bowed. "Greetings," they said in unison. We walked passed them and into the mansion.

I looked up at the huge crystal chandelier and smiled. "It's beautiful." The room was decorated in warm tones with hundreds of pictures of wolves and people hanging on the walls.

A male voice spoke from the stairway. "It better be beautiful. I paid an arm and a leg for it."

I looked up and saw the alpha from the forest wearing slacks and a button up shirt. He was handsome and his power radiated off of him in waves. He was the most powerful wolf I had ever met. He *had* to be a born wolf. I dropped my head and fought to keep my legs under me.

Sean cleared his throat. "Thomas, meet Rose. Rose, this is Thomas, our alpha."

Thomas made his way down the stairs and inhaled. His magic disappeared in an instant, and before me stood a simple man. He was *very* powerful. He held out his hand and smiled. "Nice to meet you, Rose. Sean's been telling me a lot about you."

I didn't want to be rude, but I wasn't sure about him yet. I kept my hand in Sean's and stepped a millimeter away to shake Thomas' hand. "Nice to meet you."

Thomas released my hand, and I stepped back next to Sean. I hated being so frightened, but I hated being so dependant on Sean more.

Thomas smiled at me and waved towards a room to the right. "Let's go to my study. The others are waiting."

I tensed and Sean rubbed his thumb across my knuckles. "The others want to hear your story about how the males were in your pack."

I swallowed, and Thomas smiled at me. "I promise that none will harm you here."

I didn't want to do it, to be surrounded by dominants, but his promise was sincere. I just hoped that they all kept their word. I let Sean lead me into the large room that was more suitable as a living room than a study, and stared at the five other males in the room. They were old. I could feel it as soon as I entered the room. Power vibrated around them all and I knew they were holding in their true amount of power as Thomas was. It frightened me beyond words. They were all seated on expensive looking couches that formed a circle around the edge of the room looking calm and relaxed. Sean led me to an open loveseat and sat down beside me on it to face the others. The men all smiled sweetly at me, but I couldn't find a smile to give them in return.

Thomas sat down in a chair to my right and smiled. "Rose, *calm down.*" His magic wrapped around me, even stronger than Sean's, and I was instantly relaxed. I relaxed back into my seat and Sean relaxed next to me. Thomas nodded in approval. "Alright. Now, what pack are you from?"

"Miami South," I answered quickly.

Thomas frowned. "I wasn't aware that there was a pack in Miami South. How long has the pack been there?"

I shrugged. "They didn't feel old like you do, no offense, but I was in their pack for three years."

Thomas asked, "How did you become a wolf?"

"I was bitten."

The others seemed to grow still as they listened to me.

Thomas asked softly, "And why did you leave your pack?"

I fought the fear that boiled up and tried to constrict my throat. Sean stroked my arm softly and I exhaled, spitting the words out quickly, "They beat and raped me, and I couldn't take it anymore."

The anger level skyrocketed, making me whimper. Thomas exhaled and the anger dissipated. Thomas asked, "What did the alpha do to calm those that beat you?"

I shook my head. "He didn't calm them, ever. He didn't stop them from beating or raping me either. He watched." I whispered the last part and blinked back the tears.

Sean whined and I rubbed my face against his shoulder to wipe the tears that had fallen.

One of the males sitting on the largest couch asked, "Why did they beat you?"

"They said I didn't smell right anymore and that I did too many things wrong. They told me that women are only for their amusement and I wasn't amusing them appropriately."

Thomas asked, "Where did you change?"

I looked up at him as I answered. "A cage with silver bars."

Thomas's eyes widened. "Every time?"

I nodded my head. "Every time. They said I wasn't controlled enough to change near them."

Thomas asked, "How long ago did you leave them?"

"Four years. I broke the pack ties three and a half years ago."

The males seemed shocked by my answer and the male who had spoken earlier asked, "How did you break them?"

I looked at Sean and he nodded to go ahead and answer. He was probably curious himself, since I hadn't told him this part. "I found a newly made vampire and let him bind me to him, and then killed him."

Thomas smiled, apparently entertained by my answer. "How did you know you could do that?"

"I had heard the males talking about a rumor that it could be done. It was my last resort, since I couldn't kill myself."

Thomas frowned. "You tried to kill yourself?"

I let a few tears drop before looking up at him. "I couldn't go back and let them keep hurting me. They almost killed me a few times. They killed my family. After I left, the alpha started calling me back and I tried to resist...the wounds healed too fast for me to bleed out though. Even silver wouldn't keep the wounds open long enough."

Thomas asked, "What were the males like?"

I sniffed and wiped my nose, feeling like a weak pup. "They were always angry. Anything set them off. And the alpha...I didn't even know that dominants could soothe like you did, until Sean did it on me. That alpha never did that. He would provoke them more times than not. He liked watching them fight each other or hurt me."

Thomas asked, "Have you been solo since you left them and broke your ties?"

I nodded.

He sighed. "Alright. That's all we needed to ask you. Thank you for answering our questions."

Sean licked the tears off my face and I giggled as his tongue tickled me. Sean asked, "Can she stay here tonight?"

Thomas looked at the others and then smiled. "Of course."

Sean smiled and dragged me from the chair by my hand.

"Thank you," I said. I only had time to wave to the others before he pulled me out of the room and up the stairs. I started tripping because he was pulling me too fast and he picked me up, flying up the last few stairs.

He pushed open his bedroom door and set me down on my feet. "Welcome to my room."

The floor was perfectly clean and the carpet shined as though he never stepped on it. There wasn't a blank spot on the wall, hand drawn pictures covered every square inch. I looked at the closest drawing and gasped. "Is that me?"

Sean nodded. "I drew it that first night I saw you."

I touched the picture and smiled. "You're amazing."

He picked me up and I wrapped my legs around his waist. "No, you're amazing." I kissed his lips and he sighed happily. "See, I told you everything would be okay." I laid my head down on his shoulder and he walked us over to the bed. It shocked me that I was so complacent with him now, but I felt different. Was it because he broke the mate bond? Whatever it was, I just hoped he wouldn't change.

I closed my eyes as he climbed on with me and he poked my stomach. I giggled and he laughed. "You're ticklish?"

I opened my eyes and shook my head. "No."

He heard the lie and started tickling me.

I laughed and squirmed, trying to get away from his hands when someone opened the door.

Sean spun around and growled. Fear consumed me and I cowered behind him.

I peeked around to see a man in his early twenties leaning against the door frame. "Whatcha got there, Sean?"

Sean growled again. "Leave, Patrick."

Patrick smiled and then waved at me. "Hi there."

I smiled. "Hello."

Patrick inhaled and his eyes widened. "You found a female wolf? Oh, come on let me see her."

Sean growled again and I felt his wolf stir. "Leave my room."

Patrick squatted down in an attack stance and would have attacked if Thomas hadn't grabbed his shoulder. "I believe Sean asked you to leave his room."

Patrick stood upright and backed away. "Sorry. Sorry. Leaving now."

Sean waited until Patrick was walking down the stairs before sitting back on the bed and pulling my arms around his shoulders. I kissed his ear, hoping he would calm down if I touched him. His shoulders slowly relaxed and Thomas smiled. "Maybe you should keep your door closed and keep her up here tonight."

Sean nodded his head. "Alright."

Thomas looked at me and frowned. "I called Fenrir." He noticed my confused look and asked, "You do know who Fenrir is, right?"

I shook my head.

"Fenrir is the head of all werewolves. The alpha of alphas or king of kings if you will. I asked him about your pack and he said he had no knowledge of a pack living in Miami South. He's going to investigate the matter and get back to me, but I advised him of their hostile nature. He's sending his best dominants to talk to them. Until I hear back from them I would like it if you stayed here."

I frowned. "I need to go to work—"

Thomas shook his head. "Fenrir gave me specific orders to keep you here. I'll call Mr. Smith and speak to him. I'm sure he will manage without you for a few days."

Sean asked, "Will Fenrir send her back?"

Thomas sighed. "I don't know what Fenrir will do, but I don't think he'll send her back to a pack that's been abusing her. He will not allow her to be solo though."

I nuzzled Sean's neck and he asked, "Can she join our pack?"

Thomas frowned. "I'll have to think about it. Have you discussed mating?"

I froze and Sean patted my hand. "No, we haven't discussed it."

I moved away from Sean and sat against the wall. Mating? Joining a pack? Could I do that? Would it work? What if Sean turned out to be just like Jeff? I shook my head. No, Sean isn't angry like Jeff. But... But he had gotten angry when Patrick came by.

Thomas sighed. "Rose, *calm down*."

I let his magic calm me and rolled on to my side on the bed.

Thomas sighed again. "Lock the door." I heard the door shut and then Sean got off the bed.

He climbed back on the bed slowly and settled behind me draping one arm across my waist. "Rose?"

"Hm?"

He rolled me over and smiled. "You don't have to think about the mating thing, okay? Let's just enjoy being together."

I rolled over again, so that I was lying on my left side facing him. He laid down on his back and I rested my head on his chest. "You're worried too, I can smell it."

Sean nodded. "I don't want them to try to take you away from me."

I draped my hand across his upper chest. "I don't think I could handle leaving you."

He kissed my head. "Let's not think about it." He hummed softly and I quickly fell asleep.

Chapter 8

Sean kissing me on the cheek woke me up from my pleasant dream about chasing a rabbit.

I looked up into his eyes and he smiled. "Morning."

I stretched and he bent down to kiss my exposed stomach, making me gasp and making my pulse race.

He frowned. "Rose, I promised I wouldn't ever hurt you."

I nodded. "I know, but I've heard a lot of false promises. I'm sorry. I'm trying."

He smiled. "That's all I can ask for. Come on, let's eat."

"I thought I wasn't allowed out?" I asked in shock.

He laughed. "No, he meant to keep you here when he's not nearby. Everyone eats together in the mornings. Come on or we'll be late and there won't be any food left." I stood and he led me to a bathroom. "Go on, but hurry. My toothbrush is the green one."

I walked inside the bathroom and stared at the golden veined marble. I climbed into the shower and stared at the showerhead which looked like it was made out of gold. I flicked my tongue out and my eyes widened at the taste of gold. This pack had some serious money. I would never have even dreamed of a golden showerhead.

I shook my head and quickly used the restroom and Sean's toothbrush. Luckily, I'm not one to get freaked out about using someone else's toothbrush. We already swapped spit a few times, and he rinsed the toothbrush out for heaven sakes. After I finished, Sean brushed his teeth, then held my hand as we walked down the stairs. He turned left down the hallway and then right into the biggest dining room I'd ever seen. More chandeliers and white marble with black veins made the room look like it should be in a movie about a princess, not a mansion full of werewolves.

Thirty males and five females sat around a table large enough to fit fifty. Sean took me to a seat beside Thomas who smiled at me as we came in. I tried to smile back at him, but I think it ended up being more of a grimace. Every eye was on me as I took my seat between Thomas and Sean making my skin twitch nervously. Ten of the thirty present were under the age of twenty, which surprised me. Three human girls looked at me curiously and I looked back at them with the same curiosity.

I wanted to ask them questions, but Thomas cleared his throat. "As you can all see, we have a visitor staying with us. This is Rose, and I expect you all to treat her with the utmost respect and kindness. Sean is her appointed guardian so unless you want to challenge Sean, I suggest you leave her alone. Now, let's eat."

It was only then that I noticed the piles of food on the table. Sausage, pancakes, eggs, bacon, waffles, cooked ham and what smelled like fresh squeezed orange juice.

Thomas must have seen my eyes widen because he frowned at me. "I take it you never ate like this with your pack?"

I shook my head. "I got raw steaks and lumpy, cold oatmeal

tossed in my cage twice a day. Sometimes I'd get an apple, but that was only if I..." I looked at the young girls at the table and blushed. "Well you get the picture."

Thomas asked through gritted teeth, "Is that why you are so thin?"

I frowned. "No, I just don't have enough money for food. I eat enough for a human, but..." I shrugged. "Sean stocked my cabinets yesterday, though."

Thomas nodded his head. "Good. Alright everyone eat, eat." He waved his hand and everybody started piling food on to their plates. I sat still, waiting until everyone was done for my turn. Technically I wasn't more submissive than the young girls, especially since they were human, but I was a guest and it didn't seem right to eat before them.

Thomas and Sean were frowning at me when I looked at them.

"What did I do?" I asked.

Sean looked at Thomas. "She always does this."

"If you stay with us you're going to have to be re-taught everything. If your alpha says to eat, then you eat. There is no dominant to submissive line at a food table, you just eat," Thomas explained.

"Oh, okay." I started shoveling food on my plate and the conversations began around the tables. The food was delicious and I didn't try to talk as I ate my meal. It felt strange to be sitting with so many werewolves and yet not feel scared, but I didn't question it and just enjoyed it.

As soon as everyone was done Thomas whispered, "One. Two. Three. Not it!"

Sean and I yelled, "Not it," at the same time and a few others answered after us. It was a game my family had played when I was a child. Whoever was the last had to do the dishes or whatever chore we were avoiding.

One of the older males down at the end was the last to say anything and groaned. "Dammit!"

Thomas smiled and stood. "Looks like it is Ralph's turn to clean the dishes."

Sean grabbed my hand, pulling me up and started to lead me back to his room.

Thomas called up to us, "Sean, what we talked about earlier? Don't try it with the smaller ones awake, please."

Sean actually blushed and shook his head. "Don't worry about that."

I realized what he was talking about and blushed too. "No, not that."

Sean pulled me up the rest of the stairs and into his room. "Sorry about that. He means well."

I sat down on his bed and looked up at Sean's troubled face. "What is it?" Had I done something wrong?

He shook his head and smiled, "Just thinking. Do you want to go for a run?"

I smiled. "As a wolf?"

He shook his head. "Thomas won't let you change."

I frowned. "Won't let me change? Why not?"

He sat down beside me. "Because you're not pack. He's not worried about you, but about the others trying to hurt you. Come on let's go for a run."

I sighed. "Fine." Running in human form wasn't as fun as wolf, but it was still a way to let out excess steam.

He stroked my cheek softly, and then kissed my lips. "You're cute when you're mad."

I jerked away from him and stood, my heart beating a mile a minute. Jeff's face flashed in front of my face with him doing the same thing, but I had been chained up at the time he had said those words.

I wrapped my arms around myself and whimpered as I

recalled the pain. Ten strands of wolf fur grew out of my hands as my wolf fought to take control to protect me.

Sean reached out towards me and I snapped my teeth at him, moving farther away.

"Stay back," I whispered as I tried to control my wolf side and keep from changing.

Sean held up his hands and stepped back. "What did I do?"

I inhaled and cleared my head of any thoughts. My fear dissipated, the fur disappeared and I turned back to face Sean. "Please don't say that *ever* again."

Sean walked slowly towards me with his head bowed and wrapped his arms around me. "Sorry," he whispered as he licked my chin.

I relaxed into him and inhaled his smell. He still smelled of peppermint. "It's not your fault. Sorry I snapped at you."

He kissed my cheek softly. "Come on, let's go for a run."

I nodded, but stayed silent. I couldn't mess up with Sean. He was too perfect for me to be so imperfect. I knew that I was acting strange even for me and I wasn't sure if it was a good thing or not.

Thomas made me feel like a kid, not in a bad way, but like I was protected and didn't need to be a mature adult. Was it some type of spell? Or was this how a true alpha made those of their pack feel?

Sean led me out of the room and down the stairs. Two males in their late teens stood from the floor they had been sitting on, and smiled at us. They were twins, identical twins, with blonde hair and blue eyes. They were submissives and surprisingly I wasn't nervous near them. Was Sean right about me being a dominant?

The one on the right spoke. "Hey, Sean. Where you going?"

Sean put his arm around my waist, and smiled. "For a run, you two want to join us?"

I should have been offended at the possessive gesture, but for some reason Sean's arm around my waist felt soothing. Had he done it because he was worried I'd be nervous near the twins?

The twins nodded. The one that had spoken before asked, "We changing?"

Sean shook his head. "No."

The twins frowned, but then turned and smiled at me, revealing their duplicate dimples.

"Where are my manners? Rose, this is Mike and Mark. Mike, Mark, this is Rose," Sean said as he gave the introductions.

Mike and Mark leaned forward and inhaled. I inhaled their scents quickly and smiled. "Hi."

They nodded once in unison then started towards the back door. Sean and I followed them, and I felt his growing nervousness. I rubbed my face against his shoulder and he smiled down at me. "I'm fine," I assured him.

Sean pushed open the back door and I gaped at the mini forest in the backyard. A small dirt path wrapped around the trees and one park bench sat just to the side of the path. Sean released my hand and jogged down the porch steps to the path, which I realized, was actually a track where Mike and Mark were waiting.

I followed him and one of the twins asked, "Fast, slow, or whatever?"

Sean looked at me and smiled wide. "Fast."

He turned to the others and I inched ahead of him without him noticing.

"Okay on the count of..."

I took off running down the track and heard their yells. They started running to catch up and I slowed to let them.

Never run from a wolf even when he's in man form. Sean caught up to me and then blew passed me. I growled and charged after him with the twins hot on my heels. We circled around the trees and I realized that the forest wasn't small at all. It continued out past the mansion's borders and the track was cut through it. I inhaled the smell of the trees, leaves, dirt and wolves near me and my wolf woke up. I pushed her food desires down and allowed her to increase our pace. Sean turned his head and his eyes widened in shock as I caught up and then ran past him. I came around the last turn and blew past the starting point, skidding to a stop on the track.

Thomas was sitting on the porch steps and stared at me with wide eyes as I started walking back.

Sean came around the bend and jogged over to us a little out of breath. "You're quick."

Thomas walked towards me with an intent look on his face.

I stopped moving, dropped my head down, and stayed as still as I could manage with my pounding heart.

He inhaled and asked, "How have you managed this type of control?"

I looked up at him and frowned. "What do you mean?"

He waved his hand at my face. "Your wolf side is active, your eyes are gold, and yet you aren't changing."

I shrugged. "I just subdued my wolfie food urge and allowed myself to run instead. I compromised with myself. No food, but fast running to beat the other wolves. We like beating the other wolves."

He smiled. "That type of control is very hard to gain. I'm impressed."

I bowed my head. "Thank you."

Sean smiled at me. "You're incredibly fast, probably the fastest here."

Memories of days spent running through the forest flew across my eyes before I could stop them.

In a small voice I said, "You learn to run fast when beasts pursue you."

Sean put his arm around my waist and I pulled away from him. I was acting like a teenage girl and I needed to stop.

The phone rang inside the house and Thomas left to go answer it. Sean had started talking to the twins so I started walking away slowly. "I've got to use the restroom. I'll be right back," I said over my shoulder. Sean waved at me and I continued inside. I slowed my breathing and calmed my heart beat as I walked inside the house. I was good at being invisible when I needed to be. I'd spent years trying to make myself invisible. I crept towards Thomas' study and would have jumped for joy at the fact that no one else was around if I could have. Instead, I leaned against the outside wall of his study and listened to his conversation.

"Yes, Fenrir, the girl is still here." He paused for a long time as the man on the other end spoke to him. The voice was too soft for me to be able to hear, though. "Are you sure? She seemed to be telling the truth about her experiences with that pack. All of my dominants listened in with me, and we all felt her speech as truth."

My entire body went still, not even my heart seemed to beat as I listened to the next words.

"Of course I don't doubt you, Fenrir. She must have spent a long time convincing herself of those lies to make them truth to her. We'll keep her here until her pack arrives to take her back with them."

Pack arrives to take me back!

My wolf was instantly on alert. It was time to go. I had spent too long in this place. I should have known that they would send me back. I stood to head towards the door and heard Sean laugh. My heart seemed to rip in half as I thought of leaving him behind.

I have to do it. I have to survive.

My wolf and I agreed on one thing, survival was the most important thing. I ran out the front door and didn't stop running. I could run for two days straight as a human and two additional days once I changed forms.

Thomas would have heard the door open, so he would be sending wolves after me if the guards weren't already following, but I had a head start, no matter how small it was, any bit helped.

My cell phone rang and I pulled it from my pocket and answered as I swerved around humans walking on the sidewalks and cars driving down the street. "Hello?"

"Rose, where did you go?" Sean asked, his voice frantic.

My heart tore a little at the sincerity of his worry for me. Why had I answered the phone anyways? "I'm sorry, Sean. I shouldn't have stayed. I can't go back to that pack. They lied to your Fenrir. I don't know how, but they did. I wouldn't lie about something as serious as that. I'm sorry I couldn't say goodbye. I...I..." I shook my head trying to maintain control, but the words came out anyways, "I love you."

I snapped the phone in half before tossing it on the ground and growling. It had been a long time since my wolf had spoken for me. I did not understand why she had chosen to say those last three words to him, but it was done with now and I could not take them back.

Tears streamed down my face as I ran through the town, finally making it out to the freeway. I ran along the shoulder of the freeway for thirty miles before needing to switch freeways to head east. If I could run northeast, then I might be able to bypass Jeff and his pack. They were excellent trackers, but they wouldn't know the exact course I would be taking.

As soon as the sun had fully set, I stopped at a gas station just off the freeway and begged a man for some change to get a bottle of water. I knew I had scared him, because I was sweating and covered in dirt and I was sure my eyes were wolf eyes, but he didn't scream or run away so I gave him a kiss on the cheek. That only seemed to freak him out more though, so after guzzling down the water in the bottle I started running again, getting back on the freeway and running along the center divide.

As the sun rose the next day, I decided to rest in a small wooded area just off the highway. I wasn't sure what town I was even in, or even what state, but I felt sure that I was far enough away to be able to rest. I lay down in the shade of a large oak tree and started preparing myself to change. I could run for another day as a human, but I was faster as a wolf and my senses keener. I pulled my shoes off, which were now able to speak on their own, and tossed them aside. They landed with a strange thud and I looked up to see two men smiling at me, the shoes having hit them.

"Hello, Rosie," said the shorter man.

I jumped up to run away, but a third man grabbed me from behind and slammed my back against the tree. "No, no no. You've been running from us for long enough. Now it's time for you to take your punishment."

The silent man stepped forward and my heart began racing. He was handsome. No matter how cruel or evil he was, Jeff would always be handsome. He lifted his hand and I closed my eyes, waiting for the hit, but he simply rested his hand against my cheek softly. "Hello, darling. I've missed you."

I opened my eyes and looked at the face of my ex-mate. "I can't say I've missed you, because I haven't."

Jeff smiled and then slapped me in the face, making me whine in pain. "You would think after all of the times we beat you, that you would learn to keep your mouth shut."

This is why they were here. They were going to finally kill me. They must be really mad that Fenrir found out about them. If I made them mad enough, I could make them kill me quickly, instead of torturing me. That was the best way to die.

Jeff balled up his fist and punched me in the stomach, making me gasp for air. I felt a strange tingling in my head, it had been there ever since I had let Sean stay the night and he had broken my mate bond.

Remembering Sean made me whine again.

I'm sorry Sean. I hope you won't mourn me too long.

Jeff pushed me upright and I watched as his hand changed to a paw. He slashed his claws down my arm slowly, inch after inch, making me scream in pain. The other men laughed and their eyes changed to gold as they watched. Jeff hit me in the face sideways, breaking my nose.

"You were always so uncreative in your torturing. Just as uncreative as you were in bed," I said as I looked at each man. "It's no wonder none of you have mates. I wouldn't want to mate with you if we were the last werewolves on earth."

The man holding me took my forearm in his hands and snapped it like a twig. Black spots covered my vision. I had forgotten how painful everything was. I had forgotten how much pain I could endure.

Jeff's claws pierced my stomach as he stabbed them into me. The last man stepped forward and kicked my shin, cracking the bone. I fell to my knees and felt the hot tears falling down my face just as I felt my hot blood leaking down my arm and nose and dripping from my stomach. I would be unconscious soon. I had to get them to kill me before I went unconscious.

"You always knew…how to treat a lady," I whispered.

The tingling in the back of my skull intensified as I lost blood. My body started shaking as I tried to change forms. Jeff grabbed me by the hair and pulled my head back. "None of that." Cold air wrapped around my body as he held me in human form. It was the worst feeling ever, worse than having a bone broken, worse than being raped. To not be allowed to change forms was the ultimate torture.

Everything was black, but I could still hear. It would be over soon. Jeff would have to kill me or I would change forms. Jeff squatted down beside me and whispered into my ear, "It's a shame I have to kill you. You're beautiful and I am sure we could have had beautiful kids, but now…now you must die."

Sean. I'm sorry. I love you.

"Let her go," said a familiar voice.

Sean? No, Sean couldn't be here. He couldn't have found me. I must be dead. No, Sean's not dead so he couldn't be here. I must be dreaming.

Jeff released me, letting me fall to the ground. "Who the fuck are you?"

Sean growled loudly. "You have ten seconds to step away from Rose before I tear your hearts from your chests."

I had to be dreaming. It was the only explanation. My body bucked and then my wolf took over, changing forms. I howled in pain as I finished changing and lay on my stomach as the bones started trying to repair themselves.

One of the men beside me stomped on my uninjured back leg, breaking it.

Sean growled loudly and then all hell broke loose. I could barely open my eyes to be able to see what was going on, but I could hear the growls, the sounds of fists hitting flesh, and the sounds of claws tearing skin. The metallic scent of blood clogged every other sense and forced me to open my eyes.

If Sean died for me, I had to be able to see him one last time.

I opened my eyes, and stared in shock at two dead wolves beside me and Sean holding Jeff by the throat.

"I knew she didn't lie about how you treated her. I knew she was telling the truth," Sean whispered as he continued to choke Jeff.

Thomas stepped into my view and whispered, "Sean, put him down."

Sean growled, but set Jeff down.

Jeff rubbed his throat and whispered, "Good boy." Jeff jumped away from Sean and grabbed me in a headlock.

I struggled against him, but my bones were still broken and I hd lost a lot of blood so I was still too weak. "I don't know what relationship you have with her, but Rose is mine."

Sean smiled smugly. "Actually, she's not yours. You two are no longer mated."

Jeff stopped moving for a minute as he tried to find the bond that no longer existed. Jeff looked down at me and asked, "Why would you do this, Rose? Why would you break our mating bond?" He sounded genuinely sad and hurt. He really was a psychopath. Jeff growled loudly and yelled, "You can't have her. She's mine! She's mine to beat. Mine to torture. Mine to *kill*."

His arms constricted around my throat and I looked at Sean one last time.

At least he came for me and sees that I didn't lie. I closed my eyes and exhaled, ready to die.

Sean growled and then Jeff was no longer touching me. I heard a wet ripping sound, Jeff screamed, and then there was only the sound of Sean's heavy breathing.

I opened my eyes and stared in shock at Jeff's lifeless body with a giant hole in his chest. I looked up to find Sean holding Jeff's heart in his hand.

He had killed Jeff.

Jeff was dead!

I was alive!

Thomas started to move towards Sean, but Sean growled at him. Thomas stopped moving and whispered, "I am Alpha."

Sean stopped growling and dropped his head in submission, but I could see the defiance in his posture.

Thomas walked forward again and held out his hand for the heart.

Sean shook his head and stepped around Thomas to me.

Thomas stayed where he was, watching Sean with worry lines creasing his forehead.

Sean dropped to his knees on the ground and set Jeff's heart in front of my snout as a gift. He cleared his throat and shook his head a few times before his eyes finally returned to their normal hazel color and he could say, "I love you, too."

Epilogue

Sean and I sat together on the couch of the pack's house. A week after Sean had killed Jeff, I had officially accepted the offer to join his pack.

Thomas had contacted Fenrir, advising him of the truth of my former pack. Not even a week later, Fenrir wiped out the pack.

Should I have felt bad about them being killed?

Probably.

Did I?

Not even a little bit.

Sean and I were now mated, and I was the happiest I had ever been.

I still had issues, but like he had promised, Sean was helping to heal me. I wasn't sure I would ever be completely healed, but I was healing, and that was what mattered.

"I love you," I whispered to Sean as I cuddled against his side.

He bent, kissed me lightly on the lips, and whispered, "I love you, too."

About the Author

Catherine Banks is a USA Today Bestselling fantasy author who writes in several fantasy subgenres under two pseudonyms. She began writing fiction at only four years old and finished her first full-length novel at the age of fifteen. She is married to her soulmate and best friend, Avery, who she has two amazing children with. After her full-time job, she reads books, plays video games, and watches anime shows and movies with her family to relax. Although she has lived in Northern California her entire life, she dreams of traveling around the world. Catherine is also C.E.O. of Turbo Kitten Industries™, a company with many hats including being a book publisher and Etsy store full of nerdy fun.

facebook.com/catherinebanksauthor

twitter.com/catherineebanks

amazon.com/author/catherinebanks

bookbub.com/authors/catherine-banks

Also by Catherine Banks

Song of the Moon (Artemis Lupine, Book One)

Kiss of a Star (Artemis Lupine, Book Two)

Healed by Fire (Artemis Lupine, Book Three)

Taming Darkness (Artemis Lupine, Book Four)

ARTEMIS LUPINE THE COMPLETE SERIES (Books 1-4)

Pirate Princess (Pirate Princess, Book One)

Princess Triumvirate (Pirate Princess, Book Two)

Mercenary (Little Death Bringer, Book One)

Protector (Little Death Bringer, Book Two)

Royally Entangled (Her Royal Harem, Book One)

Royally Exposed (Her Royal Harem, Book Two)

Royally Elected (Her Royal Harem, Book Three)

Royally Enraged (Her Royal Harem, Book Four)

True Faces (Ciara Steele Novella Series, Book One)

Barbaric Tendencies (Ciara Steele Novella Series, Book Two)

Demonic Contract

Anja's Secret

Daughter of Lions

Centaur's Prize